Swim at [barcode]

We had come out

Hisako daintily kicked off her shoes. "Shall we walk near the water?"

Sure, why not? The longer I stayed with Hisako, the less time I had to spend behind the desk. We strolled barefoot along the firm sand where waves lapped the shore, detouring inland when we came across one of the rock piers. Just being that close to the ocean soothed my agitation.

Until Hisako stopped dead in her tracks. She pointed to the shoreline ahead. "What is that?"

I shielded my eyes and squinted. Something large had washed up on shore. A log maybe.

No, it was a person.

Panic washed over me. I stood paralyzed for a second before my lifeguard training kicked in. I sprinted toward the body. As I drew closer, I could tell it was a woman. Her hair lay tangled about her head like seaweed, matted with sand. Her pale skin was mottled, and her lips were an odd color of blue.

My heart sank right down to my stomach. The ground seemed to tilt beneath my feet. I could hardly breathe. I dropped to my knees beside her. The ties of her halter-top bikini were tangled tight about her neck. My hands trembled as I tried to loosen them.

OTHER SLEUTH BOOKS YOU MAY ENJOY

COMING SOON FROM LINDA GERBER

Death by Latte

Death by Denim

DEATH BY BIKINI

LINDA GERBER

SLEUTH
S P E A K
An Imprint of Penguin Group (USA) Inc.

Acknowledgments

I'm deeply indebted to all the people who have had a hand in bringing this book to life.

Heartfelt thanks to my long-suffering family and their willingness to be ignored, wear mismatched socks, and eat out. GUSH to my CPs Jen, Ginger, Nicole, Barb, Julie, Marsha, Karen, and Kate!

And, of course, there wouldn't be a book without the hard work of the entire Puffin team. I still pinch myself at my incredible good fortune to work with you all. Thanks much, Theresa and Linda, for the fabulous cover design! Gracias Grace for your editorial eyes. And Angelle, as always, I appreciate your guidance and wisdom more than I can say.

SLEUTH / SPEAK
Published by the Penguin Group
Penguin Group (USA) Inc., 345 Hudson Street, New York, New York 10014, U.S.A.
Penguin Group (Canada), 90 Eglinton Avenue East, Suite 700,
Toronto, Ontario, Canada M4P 2Y3 (a division of Pearson Penguin Canada Inc.)
Penguin Books Ltd, 80 Strand, London WC2R 0RL, England
Penguin Ireland, 25 St Stephen's Green, Dublin 2, Ireland (a division of Penguin Books Ltd)
Penguin Group (Australia), 250 Camberwell Road, Camberwell, Victoria 3124, Australia
(a division of Pearson Australia Group Pty Ltd)
Penguin Books India Pvt Ltd, 11 Community Centre, Panchsheel Park, New Delhi - 110 017, India
Penguin Group (NZ), 67 Apollo Drive, Rosedale, North Shore 0632, New Zealand
(a division of Pearson New Zealand Ltd.)
Penguin Books (South Africa) (Pty) Ltd, 24 Sturdee Avenue, Rosebank, Johannesburg 2196, South Africa

Registered Offices: Penguin Books Ltd, 80 Strand, London WC2R 0RL, England

This Sleuth edition published by Speak, an imprint of Penguin Group (USA) Inc., 2008

1 3 5 7 9 10 8 6 4 2

Copyright © Linda Gerber, 2008
All rights reserved
LIBRARY OF CONGRESS CATALOGING-IN-PUBLICATION DATA
Gerber, Linda C.
Death by bikini / by Linda Gerber.
p. cm.
Summary: Sixteen-year-old Aphra Behn Connolly investigates why her father let an unknown family stay at their exclusive tropical island resort, who strangled a famous rock star's girlfriend with her own bikini top, and what a smoldering teenaged guest is hiding.
ISBN: 978-0-14-241117-9 (pbk.)
[1. Resorts—Fiction. 2. Murder—Fiction. 3. Fathers and daughters—Fiction.
4. Islands—Fiction. 5. Mystery and detective stories.]
I. Title.   PZ7.G293567Dec 2008   [Fic]—dc22   2007046771

Speak ISBN 978-0-14-241117-9

Printed in the United States of America

For Aaron. I love you.

DEATH BY BIKINI

prologue

He's coming.

I climb harder, but rain weighs down my clothes and stings my eyes. The downpour slicks decomposing leaves beneath my feet so that I slip and stumble up the hill. My thighs burn. My chest is hot and tight. I want to stop and catch my breath, but his footsteps crash steadily through the undergrowth below me.

Close. So close.

Inches from my head, a banana leaf jumps and rips apart. Half a breath later, a bullet splinters the palm trunk beside me. I drop to the ground, the sound of my scream caught in my throat. I swear I can feel the vibration of his footsteps coming nearer.

If only I could rewind the past three days, I'd do everything different. I would tell Seth I'm sorry. I would protect Bianca. I would do whatever it took to see my mom one last time before I die.

CHAPTER
1

Until last week, my most pressing concern had been getting ready to visit my friend Cami back home in South Carolina. On Friday, all of that changed. Not the part about going to see Cami; I still planned to do that. Let's just say I picked up a few more concerns along the way.

As days go, Friday had been normal . . . the last normal day I can remember. But with Friday evening came a string of events that, while they may have seemed unremarkable at the time, changed my quiet island life forever.

It all started when my dad had asked me to meet a new guest at the helipad. Nothing unusual about that— although we don't get many of them in the off-season. Guests, I mean. The late July heat can be brutal on the island, and those who know usually wait until the trade winds return before they flock back to the resort. Still, a new arrival here and there was to be expected.

I stood sweltering in my uniform, even as the sun hung low on the horizon, waiting for her on the hilltop as the helicopter set down.

Frank—our pilot—saluted as he brought the landing

skids down inside the painted circle. I sighed with relief at the breeze created by the wash of the rotors and
waved back at him. Because of our remote location, the
only way to and from the resort is by helicopter, so Frank
is like our lifeline to the city. He delivers everything—
mail, supplies, and guests.

I tried to smooth my hair as the rotors wound to a
stop. Frank climbed from the cockpit. "Hey, darlin'! You
doin' the honors tonight, eh?"

"You got it." It's not like he had to ask; the new guest
was a lady from Japan, and as Frank knew, my Japanese
was much better than my dad's. In fact, I served as the
liaison for most of our international guests—owing
to the fact that I can speak more than five languages,
whereas my dad is fluent only in French. I'll admit that
most of what I know is pretty basic, but it's enough to
check someone in.

Frank helped the lady from his helicopter and re-
trieved her suitcases from the cargo hatch while she
stood, predictably, admiring the view. It's the first thing
any new arrival does.

The helicopter pad rests atop a hill overlooking the
property, and, I have to admit, our resort makes a very
good first impression. It sits on a remote stretch of
shoreline sandwiched between jagged black mountains
draped in rain-forest green and a cerulean ocean that
stretches to an impossibly wide horizon. I remember

the first time I saw it, the beauty of it made me want to cry. Or maybe that was because my mom wasn't there to share it with me.

I stiffened and raised my chin. Four years and the confusion about my mom's decision still clung to me like a sour smell. I wasn't going to let it ruin another otherwise beautiful evening.

Frank and the lady approached the cart, and I bowed in greeting. "*Konbanwa. Yokoso.*" Good evening. Welcome.

She clapped her hands. "Oh! You speak Japanese, *ne?*"

"*Sukoshi.* Very little."

She introduced herself with a bow of her own. "I am Shimizu, Hisako."

I bowed again. "*Hajimemashite.* Pleased to meet you, Shimizu-*san.*"

"Please, you must call me Hisako."

Frank loaded the bags into the back of the cart while we settled in the front. He stepped back when he was done, touching a finger to the brim of his old blue-and-gold Navy cap. "Enjoy your stay, Miz Shimizu."

Tossing a good-bye wave to Frank, I swung the cart around for the return trip. "So, what brings you to our island, Hisako-*san?*"

"I study botany. I am interested in the number of plants unique to these islands."

"Oh, yes. I just did a plant unit in my biology class, so I know more indigenous species than I care to remember."

I steered the cart around a bend in the path. "If you'd like me to take you around sometime . . ."

"Yes. I believe I would like—Oh!" She threw out a hand. "Please, stop here!"

I coasted to the side of the path, where we could see the entire resort stretched out below us, backlit by deep corals, reds, and golds. The sun hovered like a flame orange ball atop the ocean and then sank quietly behind Technicolor waves. Hisako-*san* brought one hand to her heart and murmured in Japanese, "It is perfect."

I smiled in agreement and bowed to thank her. Not that I was personally responsible for the view or anything, but I did feel a certain amount of pride, being the owner's daughter and all. Of course, the resort was his dream, not mine, but no sense in letting reality spoil the moment. I forced a smile. "Just wait until you see the stars from your veranda."

The steward delivered Hisako-*san*'s luggage to her villa while I signed her in at the Plantation House. As usual, Dad took over from there and took our new guest to her villa while I watched the desk.

He hadn't been gone two minutes before the French doors slammed open again. I jumped and reached for the two-way radio from the desk in case I needed to call security, but I relaxed as soon as I saw who it was—our resident aging rock star, trying to wrestle a suitcase away from his latest girlfriend.

This, again, was nothing out of the ordinary. The girl was just the latest of a long string of girls he'd brought to the island, but she was by far the smartest of the lot—which is probably why she was constantly threatening to leave him. We'd nicknamed the pair Mick and Bianca, since both had declined to register under their real names.

Our secluded location makes us attractive to a lot of fake-namers like them—celebrities just out of rehab, adulterous politicians, trophy wives recovering from plastic surgery, you name it. They know their secrets— and identities—are safe with us.

Mick was one of our regulars—a big spender who kept a villa at the resort and flew in every other month with a different girl on his arm. Either he didn't think we noticed or he counted on our discretion. Maybe a little of both.

Bianca tugged on her suitcase. "I'm warning you!"

Mick tugged back, whining like a little kid. "Why won't you even listen to me?"

Not for the first time, I wondered what Bianca saw in him. She was a lot younger than him, but she didn't seem as star struck as the other girls he'd been with. If she didn't like something he did, she let him know. Most of the time by packing her bags while he—a rock god who used to smash amps and breathe fire onstage for a living—ran after her like a whimpering puppy.

Bianca finally wrestled her suitcase away from him.

"You promised to stop drinking. You're such a pig when you're drunk!"

"I did stop. Alls I had was a little nip." He pinched the air, weaving like Jack Sparrow. Even from where I was standing, I could smell the sickly sweet fermented smell of alcohol on him.

"I'm outta here."

Bianca marched into the lobby, and he followed unsteadily. "But, ba-a-a-be . . ."

"Don't 'babe' me!" She plopped her vintage leather handbag on the counter. "I'd like a flight out, please."

"Ah, c'mon. No more, I promise."

He plucked at her arm, but she swatted his hand away. "You promised yesterday. And the day before. You're pathetic." She turned to me. "Am I right, or am I right?"

I gave her a neutral smile and pulled her name up on the registration screen, just in case she really did check out this time. It happened that I did think she was right, but I had a strict personal policy about getting involved with our guests' lives: Don't. Getting involved led to getting attached, and getting attached led to getting hurt. Eventually, everyone leaves. It's a lot easier not to care when they do.

It was about that time that my dad—the great mediator—arrived. I was both relieved and disappointed to see him. Despite the fact that we host more celebrities than *American Idol,* not much exciting happens at our place, and at least the fight was interesting. Dad calmed the lovebirds down, and they all went out to the lanai to talk. The show was over.

He was still out there with them when Mr. Mulo walked into the lobby. Of course, I didn't know who he was then, but I did know we weren't expecting any more incoming flights that evening. Or were we? I stood with a pasted-on smile that I hoped would mask my uncertainty. "Good evening. May I help you?"

The man hesitated for a moment, scanning the lobby before he returned my greeting. The way he did that struck me as a little odd—like he was casing the joint or something. My imposter antenna shot straight up, and I watched him closely as he approached the desk.

He was a little taller than average, with salt-and-pepper hair combed back from a wide forehead. His clothes spoke of careless elegance, and he carried himself confidently. But behind his casual air was an unmistakable watchfulness. He was definitely hiding something.

"I would like to speak to Mr. Connolly, please."

I pressed my lips together. Was I imagining it, or did his midwestern nasal tone sound forced? I thought I could detect an underlying accent, but I'd have to hear him speak a little more before I could determine what it was.

I didn't get the chance, though, because, at that moment, Dad stepped back in from the lanai. He strode toward our new arrival, hand outstretched, as if he'd been expecting the guy.

"Jack Connolly. Pleased to meet you." He gave Mr. Imposter his trademark charm-the-guest grin as he pumped the man's hand. The way he was talking, I wondered if we'd had a last-minute call-in or something, but . . . no, Dad's smiling eyes betrayed confusion. Had we somehow both missed a reservation? Since Frank was the only pilot authorized to pick up and deliver at our location, and since he would never deliver anyone who wasn't cleared through us, it seemed the only explanation. And yet none of the stewards were anywhere to be seen. Who had brought the guy down from the helipad?

I picked up the two-way radio to give Frank a squawk. With Mick on the island, it wouldn't surprise me if this guy was a paparazzo. We should probably check it out before we went handing out any rooms. A slipup like that could cost us a buttload of PR.

But then the man leaned close to my dad and said something in a low voice that I couldn't hear. The smile faded from Dad's face, and the color drained right out of it. He glanced over and gave me a small shake of his head. I set down the radio.

What just happened? Did the guy threaten him? Should I call security?

I gripped the radio again, but stopped just short of raising it to my ear. What if I was wrong? Overreacting? I inched closer so I could hear the conversation and make a better judgment.

All I caught was the last part of the man's final

sentence. ". . . just for a few days, until suitable arrangements can be made."

Dad forced a smile again. "I'll see what we have available." He brushed past me to the computer and awkwardly adjusted the flat-screen monitor.

I bit my lip, watching his obvious discomfort. Computerizing the system had been my idea. He would have been much more composed opening the huge logbook and methodically turning the pages, which was something he used to do to buy himself thinking time. It had always bugged me, but now I felt guilty for having deprived him of the ritual.

I sidled up next to him and whispered, "You want me to do it?"

He glanced back at me, but he didn't say anything. It was like he didn't even see me.

"Shall I call the concierge to arrange a pickup for his luggage?"

"No. Thank you." He blinked and seemed to come to himself again. "I'll take care of them personally."

Them? I looked up.

Mr. Imposter was not alone.

CHAPTER
2

They stood just inside the door. The woman had short dark hair and striking—almost elegant—features. But I was more interested in the guy at her side. I guessed he couldn't have been much older than me, judging from the smoothness of his face and the sharp angles in his razor-cut hair. He wore a plain black T-shirt and nondescript jeans, and, unlike the older guy, he seemed completely at ease. He watched me openly, maybe even a little curiously.

I watched him right back, probably more curious than he was. We don't get many guys my age at the resort. Okay, we don't get any. Who brings their kid on a hideaway vacation? At least that's what I assumed he was. The imposter's and the lady's kid, I mean. They did look like they belonged together—father, mother, and son. The boy had his dad's height and his mom's strong cheekbones. He also had eyes the color of the midnight sea. Mr. Imposter's were plain dark brown. I decided I liked the blue eyes much better.

As if he could tell what I'd been thinking, the son's lips curved into a smile. I blinked and looked away, my face all hot and tight. I'm not used to people looking at me. I mean, really *looking* at me. Of course, I don't usually go around staring at them, either. At least not right out in the open. Working at the resort, I've learned the value of dealing with the guests as unobtrusively as possible—blending into the background.

Usually the blending part comes naturally for me since I happen to be what you might call unremarkable to look at—average height, average weight, average-length average brown hair. At a resort populated by beautiful people, all that averageness pretty much makes me invisible. But apparently not to this guy.

I straightened. What was I, twelve? I wasn't going to get all flustered just because some boy looked at me. I turned my attention back to Dad, who seemed to be in some sort of trance, staring at the blank registration screen.

"You want me to do that?" I offered again.

He stiffened and jerked his head in my direction, startled, like he'd forgotten I was there. "No! I'll take care of it, Aphra. You go on up to bed."

"But if you'd like me to—"

"I've got it." His voice took on a sharp edge. "Good night."

I took a step back, stung. Dad had never spoken to me in that tone before. He'd never treated me like a little kid. In fact, when we first moved to the resort, Dad brought me into his office and sat me down to talk. He knew how upset I'd been when I realized my mom wasn't coming with us, but he said we could get through it if we stuck together. He explained about his plans for the resort and his need for my cooperation, as if I were a business partner with whom he had to confer. "It's just you and me now, you understand? We've got a big job to do."

I took him at his word. I thought we were a team. So how could he send me to bed like some errant child? In front of guests!

"But I was just—"

"Aphra! Go!"

I spun and pushed through the French doors out into the sultry night air. My fists curled tight, and I had an overwhelming desire to slug something. Or someone. I paced the length of the lanai. The sweet perfume of the potted plumeria and jasmine—a scent I usually loved—suddenly smelled false and cloying.

Through the window, I could see the imposter and his family, waiting expectantly as Dad fumbled through the check-in. Again I wondered if Frank had flown them in. Had he even had time to get to the city and back after dropping off the last guest? I would like to have called him to ask, but there was no way I was going back to the office to get the two-way. Not with the mood Dad was in. His snappish tone replayed in my head, and I grew angry all over again.

I couldn't stay there. I had to move, to give the anger and frustration an outlet. I backed away from the window, bounded down the steps of the lanai, and tore across the manicured lawn to where the huge banyan tree dominates the northern seaward corner of the court-yard. Pushing my way through its hanging roots, I finally came out onto the beach. My beach. My sanctuary.

Our shoreline is broken up into little scallops of sand divided by natural lava rock piers that jut out into the water like prehistoric fingers. The finger on my beach comes all the way up to the tree line on one side, cutting it off almost completely from the other beaches. The banyan tree shields it from the courtyard. That, plus the fact that it's the farthest beach from where the villas are situated, means hardly anyone ever goes there. Except me.

I breathed deep the familiar, comforting tang of salt and seaweed. Waves curled gently inland, breaking in a steady *shush* across the beach. Moonlight shimmered across the foam. If the ocean couldn't calm me, nothing could. Kicking off my shoes, I dropped my shorts and shirt in the sand. Like a lot of our guests, I practically live in my swimsuit. Unlike them, I actually swim in mine. When I was younger, I spent so much time in the water that my mom called me her little fish. But I haven't been her little anything for a long, long time.

I jogged the last few yards to the shore, waded in, and dived under. The seawater cooled the fire in my face and raised goose bumps on my skin.

Following the current downward, I skimmed along the sandy bottom until my lungs burned, then I made myself stay underwater just a bit longer. That's my ritual—something I do when I need to clear my head.

Stay under long enough and pretty soon all you can think of is the primal need to breathe. It didn't work that night, though. All I was left with was an ache in my chest that had nothing to do with the lack of oxygen.

I shot back up to the surface and gasped in a huge gulp of salty air before diving under again. My ritual was failing me. I couldn't make my head cooperate.

I'd probably gone down half a dozen times before I noticed that the surf was starting to get rough. The wave height didn't usually bother me; we're on the windward side of the island, so I'm used to it, but the power of the surge was getting intense, which meant I should probably head for shore before it got too dangerous.

I swam toward the beach, riding the waves until I could touch the bottom and wade in. I stepped lightly, careful to avoid the sharp rocks that lurk beneath the sand. See, we're not Laguna or Mazatlán or any of those places where all the beaches have nicely padded sandy bottoms. Ours is a volcanic island where the waves can carry away the sand and leave the rock exposed, sharp as glass.

I was picking my way toward the beach when I saw him. Imposter Junior sat on the shore watching me.

Despite the coolness of the water, my face grew hot again. My calm facade rolled away with the waves. All I knew about teenage guys was what I had read in Cami's e-mails. I had no experience actually dealing with one.

What was he doing? Waiting for me? And then what? What was I supposed to say to him? What—

I heard the crash of the wave too late. It rammed into me like a bull elephant, knocking the breath out of me. The next thing I knew I was facedown in the surf, heavy water pummeling the back of my head. Stupid, stupid, stupid. I knew better.

Never turn your back to the ocean.

The wave receded and pulled me with it. I scrabbled at the sand, but the force of the water dragged me under and tumbled me like a washing machine. The rip current pulled me seaward.

I'm not one to panic, but I will admit I started to freak. It was dark. I didn't know which way was up or down. My chest felt like a crushed milk carton. Dizzy spots circled before my eyes. I was going to die.

Then pain sliced along my arm. *Yes!* The rocks. That way was down. I righted myself and swam sideways as hard as I could, out of the current's pull.

Finally, I was free. Pushing upward, I popped to the surface, coughing and gagging. It took a minute for my head to clear and another minute to figure out where I was. A deep chill settled in my gut as I realized the water had carried me nearly twenty feet out. Much farther and I would have been diced on the reef.

My muscles felt heavy and useless as I tried to swim toward the shore. It wasn't until I could touch the bottom to walk in that I realized the wave had nearly torn my bikini top off. I gasped and straightened it to cover myself, praying that the imposter kid hadn't noticed. But when I looked to the shore, he wasn't there. Not where he had been sitting, anyway. Another glance and I saw him splashing through the water about fifteen feet to my left. It took a second to register; that's where I had been when I went under. The fool was probably trying to save me. I didn't have the energy to signal him. I did try to call out to him, but a wave slapped the words from my lips and left me with a mouthful of salt water instead.

All I could do was adjust my course so that I would come in a little closer to where he was. It's a good thing, too, because he made the same mistake I had, and he went down next.

Fortunately for him, his wave wasn't quite as big as the one that had slammed into me. I lost sight of him in the churning white water, but then he popped up like a cork, just over an arm's length from me. He had time only to take a breath and give me a startled look before a larger wave rose above us. And I had time only to grab his shirt and pull him down to dive under the surge. He struggled against my grasp as we went underwater, and I lost him for a moment, but I managed to snag his ankle before he was pulled away.

We both surfaced at the same time, sputtering and gasping for breath.

"Why . . . did you . . . ," he wheezed.

"Lifeguard," I said, pointing to myself. I was too wiped out to explain the finer points of surf survival, so I just showed him the next swell as it began to rise. "We ... ride this one ... in. Got it?"

He nodded and followed my lead, paddling with the rush of water until it lifted us up on the crest and pushed us toward shore. I didn't have any breath left in me to tell him what to do, so I could only hope he'd bodysurfed before and could figure it out.

I concentrated on keeping my own body in a streamlined position on top of the wave. I could feel him next to me, though—and I could swear he was laughing. We rode the crest until it crashed down, tossing us and grinding us into the sand. At least there *was* sand. It would have been worse if we'd have hit rock.

Like some primordial creature, I crawled out of the water and collapsed—after checking to make sure my top was in place, of course. He dragged himself over to where I had sprawled and flopped onto his back next to me.

We lay there, not saying a word, for a long time. All I cared about in those moments was breathing in and out. My heart was still jumping around in my chest so hard it almost hurt. I stared at the stars, thinking how bright they looked. What if we had drowned? I would never have seen those stars again. Never have seen my dad. My mom ...

He broke the silence. "Some ride, huh?"

"Huh."

We lay still a little while longer, and then he said, "I'm Adam. Adam Smith."

"Aphra Connolly."

He reached over and held his hand out to me. "Thanks for the save."

I grasped his hand—weakly, I'm afraid—and shook it. "Thanks for coming in after me."

He gave me a half nod. "So. You live here?"

"Yeah."

"You like it?"

How was I supposed to answer that? No one ever cared to ask before—not my dad and especially not a guest. I loved the island, but I missed having friends to talk to. I lived for the sun and the sea, but I would trade them both in a second if I could have my old life and my family together again. Adam was waiting for an answer, but some things are too complicated to explain. I shrugged. "S'okay."

He sat up, hooking his arms around his knees. His back and broad shoulders were plastered in sand, and his dark hair was matted with it. "What do you do for fun around here?"

I propped myself up on one elbow. "That was it."

He gave me a sideways glance and then laughed. "Oh, great. Now what am I supposed to look forward to the rest of the trip?"

"How long will that be?"

He looked away. "I don't know."

"Oh." I pushed down a little quell of uneasiness. Ours was not a drop-in, stay-till-whenever type of place. People generally knew well in advance how long they were going to visit us—they had to, in order to book a villa. I thought of Adam's imposter dad and the way he'd inspected the lobby. How my dad's face froze during their whispered conversation. Something was definitely not right, but I didn't want to look at it too closely. Not tonight. Not with the moon and the sea and someone to share it with.

I took a deep breath. "If you want, I could show you around sometime."

His smile returned. "Show me around what? I thought this was it."

Touché.

"For special patrons, we offer the near-death mountain experience as well." I pointed back toward the hills.

He caught my arm and lifted it to the moonlight. "Yow. Does that hurt?"

It wasn't until I saw the scratch that the pain began to register—faintly at first, and then stinging like the salted wound it was. A deep scratch ran the length of my forearm, oozing blood that mingled pink with the seawater. "It's not too bad," I lied, "but I should probably . . ." I glanced back toward the Plantation House.

"Right." He stood with some considerable effort. "Come on. I'll walk you." He held his hand out to me again, and this time the moonlight glinted off a ring on his finger—the ugliest, gaudiest gold and garnet thing I'd ever seen. It looked out of place.

"No, it's okay. I can—" I pulled my eyes away from the ring and started to get up, but my head tingled and my vision began to darken. I sank back down onto the sand.

He bent next to me, face all serious and concerned. "Are you all right?"

"Yeah. Fine. No worries." I sat up again—slowly this time—and he wrapped an arm around my shoulders to help me.

I stiffened. Not that I wasn't enjoying the contact or anything, but all sorts of alarm bells started going off inside my head—mainly because I *was* enjoying it. The whole thing was a little too cozy. He was a guest. Likely leaving in a few days. And even if he wasn't, nothing good could come of my letting my guard down. I thought of my mom, of the friends I'd left back home, of my dad snapping at me that night. You let people get too close, you just get hurt.

He must have sensed my hesitation because he chuckled. "Don't worry. I'm harmless."

My face started to do the burning thing again. "Oh, no. I didn't mean—"

"I know. I don't usually rescue girls on a first date, either."

He looked so ridiculous with his exaggerated contrite expression that I had to smile.

His face brightened, and he helped me to my feet. He half guided, half supported me over to where my things lay in the sand. Of course he wasn't much steadier than I was, and the two of us nearly fell over more than once. By the time we reached my clothes, we could barely stand for laughing.

I pulled on my blouse, folded my shorts, and slipped my gritty feet into my shoes.

The conversation died as we picked our way through the banyan roots and up the path toward the Plantation House. When a section of the path veered off toward the villas, I stopped. "Well, good night."

"No. I can walk you all the way up."

"But don't you go this way?" I pointed down the path.

"No, our villa is off to the left up there, by the big palm tree."

"Are you sure?" That didn't make any sense. There was only one villa to the left of the Plantation House, and it wasn't ready to be occupied.

"Yeah, I'm sure. Villa four."

"Oh, no."

"What's the matter?"

"I'm so sorry. We can move you."

"Why?"

"Are you kidding?"

"It's fine."

"It's under renovation."

"Oh. I thought the plastic sheeting was part of the de-cor." It took me a second to realize he was joking. That was long enough to make him laugh.

His laughter died abruptly when Adam's imposter dad, Mr. Smith, stepped out of the shadows. "Adam!" he hissed. "Where have you been?"

Adam's face darkened. He shoved his hands into his damp, sandy pockets and whispered sideways to me, "I better go. You know how it is; spies and parents never sleep."

He left with his dad, and I stood on the path, staring long after they'd gone. I felt numb. Adam's last words buzzed in my head.

My mom used to say the *exact* same thing.

CHAPTER
3

Dad was always the careful one. Mom used to make him crazy with the things she'd do, especially when she took me with her. I learned to scuba dive when I was ten. When I was eleven, she taught me to rock climb and rappel. I was supposed to go white-water rafting with her when I turned twelve, but she left before my birthday.

I used to lie on the floor in my room at night with my ear pressed to the boards and listen to my mom and dad fight. He'd say she was being reckless with me, and she'd say I was learning to be strong. He'd make her promise to be more careful, and she'd promise she would. And then we'd try something new the next day.

"Just don't tell Dad," she'd whisper.

We'd giggle like girlfriends when we talked about each new adventure, and it made me feel important that she wanted to share the things she loved with me. Mom was always the one to kiss away a tear or patch a skinned elbow. She tucked me in at night and read me bedtime stories. And when I had nightmares, Mom would always be there as soon as I woke up. She'd crawl under the covers with me, smooth back my hair, and tell stupid jokes until I laughed. Before long, I forgot to be scared.

I once asked how she knew whenever I needed her. She just smiled and said, "It comes with the territory, hon. Spies and parents never sleep."

I skipped my usual swim in the morning and went straight to the registration desk so I could look up the Smiths' information before Dad got to the office. It's possible he had forgotten villa four was under construction when he was checking them in; he did appear to be a little distracted after Adam's dad had spoken to him. If they were legitimate guests, we should move them right away.

I ran a quick computer search but couldn't find any sign-in at all listed for villa four. I checked the filing in-box next. Sometimes when Dad gets frustrated with the computer, he just does the paperwork by hand and leaves it for me or the other staff to input.

Nothing.

He walked into the lobby while I was searching the computer files again. I looked up, trying to gauge his mood. After the way he'd snapped at me the night before, I wasn't sure where I stood.

He caught my look and gave me a smile. A forced smile, perhaps, but at least it looked like things were back to normal. Maybe. "What are you working on this morning?"

I glanced almost guiltily at the computer. "I, um . . . I was updating the client list, and I can't find the Smiths' information."

He stiffened and shot me a look I couldn't decipher. Uh-oh.

"Information?"

"The check-in. There's no record of them—"

"Don't worry about it. I took care of it."

I pasted on a smile. "Oh, good. Do you want me to enter the info into the system?"

"Thank you, but that won't be necessary."

Just like that. No explanation. He stood next to me, calmly sifting through yesterday's mail as if it were perfectly normal for him to have placed guests in a villa with plastic sheeting for walls and no kitchen floor.

I reviewed the inventory sheet for Frank's next flight, matching Dad's calm with a calm of my own. Outwardly, at least. Inside I was screaming with frustration. Did he think I was stupid? I was there when the Smiths arrived. Even if he didn't know about my meeting with Adam, he had to know I'd wonder where those people went.

The worst thing was that I couldn't pursue it any further now that he had effectively closed the conversation. I knew how stubborn he could be. I'd have to fish for information elsewhere.

"Well, I'm done for a while." I signed off on the sheet and filed it away. "Do you mind if I run over to the lounge for a minute? I want to get some bandages from Darlene."

He looked up from the mail. "Hmm? What? What's wrong?"

"Nothing, really. I just scraped my arm on some rocks this morning when I went swimming." Technically, that was not a lie. It was after midnight by the time I'd gotten back to my room, so it really had been morning. I did feel bad about the half-truth, but if he knew where I'd gone the night before, I might have forfeited my trip. We had rules against swimming after dark.

He inspected the scratch, which by then had turned a nasty, puffy umber. "You'd better have her put some disinfectant on it, too."

He turned back to the mail, and I went looking for answers.

The one person on the island who keeps up with all the gossip is our lounge manager, Darlene. She's been with us at the resort since the beginning, so she's a fixture on the property and the closest thing to family that I have. Besides my dad, that is.

Darlene isn't a nurse, but she is like the resident mom, and so she's the one in charge of the first-aid kit. I headed for the lounge and found her behind the bar, stacking glasses. As I expected, the lounge was empty—with the exception of Mick, who was sleeping in the corner, his hand half wrapped around what looked like a glass of tomato juice.

Darlene's face brightened when she saw me. "Eh, Aphra! What's the haps?"

"I need a Band-Aid."

Her smile disappeared. Small bandages we had back at the Plantation House, so if I was coming to her, she had to know it was something bigger. "Oh. Lemme see."

"It's no big deal. Dad just told me to have you look at it." I slid onto a bar stool and rested my arm on the counter.

She grabbed the first-aid box from under the bar. When she saw the scratch, she grimaced. "Ai. Does it hurt?"

"Not much."

"Then I'm sorry for this." She grabbed my hand to hold it down and then spritzed my arm with antiseptic spray. "Don' want it to get infected."

I hissed in a breath. The antiseptic stung and burned, but not a whole lot worse than the salt water had.

She measured out a gauze strip. "So why you really here?"

"I'm sorry?"

"Nah. Don' be sorry. Just tell me what's up."

Darlene, it should be said, knows me a whole lot better than my dad does. I should have figured she'd see right through me. "I just wanted to ask . . . It's probably nothing."

"What's nothing?"

I hunched my shoulders. "You know villa four? Do you know if it's still torn up?"

"It just needs cabinets and flooring now. Maybe a little paint. Why ask me? You seen it."

"Yeah, but it's been a few days, so I wondered. I just thought it was weird that Dad put the Smiths there last night."

She glanced up from wrapping my arm. "The who?"

"The family that came in last night."

She taped off the end of the gauze, frowning. "What family?"

My heart dropped. That was not a good sign. As manager of the lounge, Darlene had to know the comings and goings of all the guests so she could get their meals prepared and charged to the right villa. She should have gotten the paperwork ten minutes after the Smiths checked in, if not before. Even if Dad had somehow forgotten to send it over, he always met with senior staff first thing in the morning. Why wouldn't Dad have told Darlene about them then?

I frowned. That kind of oversight was not like him at all. He's so obsessive with paperwork and procedure, he borders on anal. "Darlene, you saw my dad this morning, right? Did he seem a little off to—"

"'Scuse me." Mick called from his table, holding an empty glass. He had apparently woken up thirsty.

Darlene pressed her lips together. "Sorry, honey. Duty calls. You make sure I get that family's info, yeah?"

I walked outside, blinking in the morning sun. Something was definitely going on. Dad hadn't been himself since the moment the Smiths showed up in the lobby. I chewed on my lip, remembering how Mr. Smith's words had stolen Dad's smile. What could he have said?

I couldn't bear to go back to the office. Not with Dad being so weird. There were too many questions to be answered. What I really needed was a long swim so I could think, but I could hardly justify going to the beach when I was supposed to be working. If I went to clean the pool, however . . .

During the slow months we operate at half staff, and I make extra money by taking on more jobs. Now that I'd earned my lifeguard certification and my hourly wage had inched up, Dad had added pool upkeep to my daily list of chores. So really, going to the pool was technically justified.

There wasn't much upkeep to do since we have an automatic filtration system and everything, but there's always a bug or two to be skimmed from the surface of the water, especially when the mosquito population reaches its peak, as it does each year when the weather turns hot.

At the pool house, I hung my shorts and blouse in the employee locker and padded barefoot out to the deck. Only a sprinkling of dead insects and a handful of leaves floated in the pool, but that was enough to warrant cleaning, right?

I grabbed the skimmer and started to fish them out when I saw Bianca strolling up the walk. She looked every bit the part of a rocker chick in a retro crocheted halter-top bikini, platform sandals, and oversize white-rimmed mod sunglasses.

"Hey, girl!" She waved as she approached. "What they got you working for on a beautiful day like today?"

I gave her a resigned smile and a you-know-how-it-is shrug and continued cleaning the pool.

She skirted the edge and dropped onto a chaise near where I was working. "Hey, you wanna take a break for a bit?" She patted the chair next to her. "I won't tell if you don't."

"Oh. Thank you, but—"

"Please. Ray's off doing his thing somewhere, so I don't have anyone to talk to. You can keep me company."

Ray was Mick's island pseudonym. The one he chose for himself, that is. I have to tell you, visiting with Bianca was tempting. She was without a doubt one of the most interesting people I'd ever met on the island. But visiting with guests was just not something I did. Be helpful, yes. Be pleasant and polite, yes. But *visit*? No, thank you. It was better just to keep my distance.

"Ah, c'mon. We can talk about that new kid you were with last night."

That was all it took. I set down my pole.

She grinned triumphantly. "I saw you from our veranda last night, coming up from the beach. He's a hottie, that one. I'd hang on to him if I were you."

I could actually feel the blush creeping across my cheeks. "It's not like that."

"It's always like that."

"He's a guest."

"And?"

"It's just . . . I don't . . ."

She winked. "Of course you don't."

I fell silent, and my discomfort must have amused her because she laughed.

"I'm just giving you a hard time. Come on. Sit." She patted the seat cushion again. "I'll play nice, I promise."

I sat.

She sighed with exaggerated contentment. "See? Isn't that better?"

I nodded.

"Nice pool."

"Thank you."

"Ooh, I love it. You're so proper and polite."

"Thank you." I gave her an elaborate seated curtsy this time, which made her laugh again.

"There it is! I knew you had a personality lurking behind the mask."

I blinked. "Mask?" Me?

"Oh, yeah. I've seen you around, acting all professional and aloof. What are you, like, seventeen?"

"Sixteen."

"Even worse. You should be out partying. Or at least not being so damn careful all the time. Believe me, life's too short."

Careful? That was my dad, not me. I was . . . smart.

Smart to toe the line with school and work. Smart not to rock the boat. Smart to maintain an appropriate distance from the guests. But that remark stung. Or hit too close to home.

I fought hard for a comeback, but nothing sprang to mind except, "At least I'm not lying around a swimming pool less than two hundred yards from the beach."

"What?" She laughed, free and happy. "Well, I suppose you've got a point. However"—she crossed her long legs—"some people don't like sand."

"What's the draw of a beach resort, then? Why not vacation in Kansas or someplace with a really great pool instead of flying three thousand miles to find the ocean?"

"They have great pools in Kansas?"

I laughed. "You know what I mean."

"So this is a pet peeve of yours, is it?"

I hesitated. Maybe I should just keep my mouth shut.

"C'mon." Bianca leaned back on the chaise, grinning. "Give it to me straight."

"Okay." I took a deep breath. "Before we came here, my dad ran a resort in South Carolina that sat on the most gorgeous beach you've ever seen. White sand, crystal clear water. But that wasn't good enough for the owners. They built a huge swimming pool up on a platform so that it looked like it spilled over into the ocean. It was pretty, but it ruined the beach—and, come on. A pool just isn't the same as the ocean. It has no energy. No life."

"So true." Bianca swung her legs over the side of the

chaise. "You know what? You've inspired me. I'm tired of waiting around for Ray. I think I'll keep it real and go to the beach. And besides"—she lowered her sunglasses—"three's a crowd."

I followed her gaze to see Adam coming down the terraced steps toward the pool. He was shirtless, in a pair of royal blue board shorts that offset his tanned skin. He moved smoothly, all broad shoulders and six-pack abs. I let out an appreciative breath.

A knowing smile spread across Bianca's face. "Now that's what I'm talking about."

"No . . . I'm not—"

She laughed and stood up. "Nice hangin' with you, kid." Sliding her sunglasses into place, she strolled off toward the beach.

Adam waved when he noticed I was watching him. He took the last few steps two at a time.

"Hi!" I waved back. "What're you up to this morning?"

"Looking for you."

I swear I must have blushed all the way up from my toenails. "Really?"

"Yeah." His gaze wandered beyond me to the deserted pool. "So is this where you guard all those lives?"

I laughed. "Yes. As you can see, it's a very demanding job."

"Is it always this busy?"

"Pretty much. When the resort's full, we get a handful of sun lizards, but that's about it."

He eyed my bandage. "How's that doing?"

"This? It's fine."

"Can you get it wet?"

"I guess."

"So . . ." He gestured with his head toward the pool.

"Oh. I can't. I'm supposed to be working."

"Ah." He looked at his feet. "Got it. Do you mind if I . . . ?"

"No, not at all."

I stepped back as he kicked off his sandals and executed a perfect dive from the side of the pool. He surfaced just as gracefully, his dark hair slicked back and dripping.

"Very nice."

He didn't answer, but sank beneath the water. A second later, he came up thrashing. "Agh! Leg cramp! Help! Help!"

I laughed. "Hold on. I'll throw you a life preserver."

He stopped sloshing. "You're no fun."

"I'm working."

"And I'm drowning. As the lifeguard, isn't it your job to save me?"

I hesitated. On the one hand, I *had* been planning on going swimming. I just hadn't planned on Adam being with me. I probably shouldn't . . . but then I remembered Bianca's mocking grin. I was being careful again. What would it hurt? If she could deal with sand between her toes, I could let myself relax a little. I closed my eyes and jumped into the pool before I could change my mind.

Once I got in the water, I remembered that I hadn't finished skimming the pool. I cringed, scooping up a mosquito carcass and flinging it onto the deck.

"That's an interesting ritual."

I spotted another bloodsucker and scooped it out as well. "I should get out and get the net."

"For what? A couple of bugs? We went swimming in the lakes all the time back home. This is nothing."

I hooked my elbows over the lip of the pool and let my legs float behind me. The cement was warm under my arms. "So, where's home?"

"Uh . . . Montana."

"Where in Montana?"

He hesitated. "Butte."

"Why the pause? Can't you remember?"

"I . . . wasn't sure you'd know where it was, you know, since you live so far away."

I swatted water at him. "I've only been here four years, and I do remember my geography, thank you very much. I learned all the states and capitals before I was six."

"Me, too," he boasted. "*And* all the major freeways."

I drew back. "Seriously? I thought I was the only weird kid who did that. My mom and I used to map imaginary road trips, and I had to figure out the distance and time traveled."

He laughed. "Wow. I was just kidding, but you really know them? That *is* weird."

Well, that deserved some kind of a comeback, but I couldn't think of one, so I splashed him. He splashed me back. I splashed him again, a little harder this time. He laughed and grabbed me, trying to wrestle me under the water. I hooked my arm around his neck so he couldn't dunk me without going down himself, but it didn't faze him. We both went under. He grinned at me, cheeks all puffed up like a double-sided balloon. I grinned right back. I'd been building my endurance for years, with my swimming ritual and all. I could outlast him.

But he was still with me when my lungs started to burn. Still with me as the ache in my chest turned into desperation. Finally, I had to break free and push for the surface. He followed, but I came up first.

"Not bad for a girl."

"Yeah? Well, I was just protecting your fragile male ego."

He laughed at that, and the conversation lulled. I took the opportunity to climb from the pool so I could dry off on one of the lounge chairs. Adam followed.

We sat quietly for a moment. I turned to him. "Hey, did our dads know each other before you got here?"

He propped himself up on his elbows. "I don't think so. Why?"

"Just wondering. The way they were talking the other night..."

"Oh. I didn't hear what they were saying. Did you?"

"No. It just seemed like they might be . . . old friends."

He shrugged. "Maybe. I don't know. Dad never mentioned it."

"How did you decide to come to our resort for your vacation?"

"That's easy. I heard you had the hottest lifeguard around, and I begged until the parents gave in."

I blushed hot and looked away.

"What? No more questions? Okay. It's my turn. Is Aphra a family name? I don't think I've heard it before."

"Well, it's not really a family name, like my aunt or grandma shares it or anything, but my mom chose it, if that counts. She named me after Aphra Behn."

"Who's that?"

"Are you kidding? Only one of *the* first professional women writers. She was also a spy for King Charles II. My mom, she used to be really into spies and stuff like that."

"Used to be? So she isn't anymore?"

"I don't know. I haven't seen her for a while. She left when we moved here."

"Oh. I'm sorry."

I picked at a seam on the chaise. Well, that was one way to kill a conversation. Which was probably a good thing because it saved him the tedium of hearing how it felt to find out at twelve years old that you are going to a new place with no friends, no school, no television, no movie theaters, no malls, no fast food, and, by the way, no mom.

"Moving sucks," he said finally. "It changes everything. Each new place, you have to reinvent yourself to suit the situation. It's like you have no control over anything."

"I know! Your whole life gets rearranged, and you're just supposed to accept it."

"Well, at least you got to move here. It's a lot better than ending up in West Bloom—" He seemed to catch himself and paused for a second. "You know, a lot of people would love to live in a place like this."

"No, a lot of people would love to *visit* a place like this. There's a difference."

"So, do you miss it? Your home before here?"

I shrugged. "I was only twelve when we left South Carolina. But I miss the things I wish I was doing."

He lowered his brows. "Okay, you're going to have to explain that one."

"I have a friend back home I've kept in touch with. Every time she e-mails me about going to the latest movie or getting her driver's license or being asked to the prom, I have serious bouts of homesickness, even though I never got to do any of those things there."

He nodded. "Well, at least you *can* keep in touch."

"What about you? You've moved, too?"

"Once or twice."

"And do you still stay in contact with your old friends?"

He shrugged. "Sometimes. Through Facebook, mostly. I don't get much chance to e-mail."

"Oh! Cami has an account too. She keeps telling me I should—"

"Aphra, may I see you for a moment?"

I jumped and twisted around. Dad! I had completely forgotten I was supposed to be working. His carefully bland expression showed he wasn't happy about it, either. He wasn't the kind to yell or scold or anything like that, but when he was disappointed in me or mad at me, I knew it. He became ultra-polite and aloof. Oh, and sometimes he docked my pay—something he couldn't get away with for the other employees. To me, losing money was worse than being grounded. He may not have been aware of it, but the cash I was saving was one day going to help me find my mom. I wanted to ask her why she left.

I stood and walked over to him with as much dignity as a kid caught playing around instead of working can muster. "Yes?"

He lowered his voice. "I've been looking all over for you. Please grab your things. You're needed in the office."

I turned and gave Adam an apologetic frown.

He nodded in understanding. "I should get going anyway. I'll see you around?"

I sure hoped so.

Dad was silent most of our walk back to the Plantation House, but as we came to the courtyard, he finally spoke. His voice was tight. "What were you doing with that boy?"

"Nothing. We were just talking."

"Well, don't. I want you to keep away from those people, understand?"

Those people? What was he talking about? "You mean his family? Why? Who are they?"

He regarded me for a second and then looked away again. "They're guests who have asked for their privacy, and I would like you to respect their wishes. Now if you would hurry and get dressed, Miss Shimizu is waiting for you in the lobby."

Right. I had offered to show her around. "Oh. Yes, of course." I hurried up to my room and changed, not even bothering to rinse the chlorine out of my hair before I pulled it back into a ponytail.

Dad's warning kept turning over in my head. *I want you to keep away from those people.* Why? What was he not telling me? The frustration built again. I ground my teeth. Why couldn't he just talk to me?

When I reached the lobby, Dad was chatting with

Hisako near the lanai doors. He looked up at me. "Ah, there you are." His voice was all sunshine and roses, as if he hadn't been angry just a few short minutes before.

I forced a smile and bowed. "Hisako-*san*. So nice to see you again."

She bowed in return. "I hope this is a good time?"

"Of course." Actually, considering Dad's moodiness, the timing couldn't be better. I really wasn't sure where to take Hisako on this little nature hike of ours, but I recognized an opportunity to escape when I saw one. I figured we could start at the far side of the property and work our way back.

We took the back path, and Hisako admired the landscaping as we walked. "It is so lovely here! I suppose you meet a lot of fascinating people in such a place?"

I hated to disappoint her, but our guests really weren't as fascinating as they thought themselves to be. "I suppose . . ."

"It is such a cozy setting. Very peaceful, and so quiet."

"Well, it's actually quieter than usual now. When we're full, it can get really busy."

"Oh? So you do not have many guests at the moment? How many are here?"

"Only a handful."

Hisako nodded politely, and I snuck a glance at her. Was she bored? We hadn't come on the walk to talk about the property; we were supposed to be talking about plants, and I was failing miserably. I had to find something worth showing her, or she might decide the walk wasn't worth her trouble. Then I'd be stuck inside. With Dad.

I directed her attention to the orange-red flowers of a koki'o hibiscus. "This is one of my favorite plants. The petals remind me of flamenco dancers fanning their skirts."

"Very beautiful." She stopped to make a quick sketch in the small blue book she carried.

We continued our walk, with me pointing out some of our finer local flora and her murmuring appreciation. She was especially taken with one of the plants—a Star of Bethlehem with its cluster of small white flowers.

"Ah, *sugoi!*" She bent to examine it. "Madam Fata plant. We have these in Japan. They are very poisonous." Her voice was almost reverent. Botanists can be very weird about their plants.

"Be careful handling it," I warned. "The sap burns if it gets on your skin."

She pressed her lips together as if suppressing a smile. "Thank you, Aphra-*chan*. I will remember that."

My ears burned, and I suddenly felt like an awkward little girl. She was the botanist, and here I was lecturing her about how to handle a plant. How lame can you get? I tried to cover my humiliation by forcing more conversation. "So . . . what got you interested in botany?"

She tilted her head to one side as if this question required serious thought. "I am interested to know what plants can do. They hold much power—to soothe, to heal, even to kill."

"Oh, yeah. We did a unit on the medicinal uses of plants in my biology class. Of course, I forgot most of it as soon as I took the final."

She laughed. "What do you remember?"

I told her how the noni and kava plants can help you sleep. In turn, she shared that the nuts of the kukui could be used as a laxative—as if I really wanted to know that—and that salvia plants have psychoactive effects.

By this time, we had reached the end of the paths and had come out onto the sand of the beach. Hisako daintily kicked off her shoes. "Shall we walk near the water?"

Sure, why not? The longer I stayed with Hisako, the less time I had to spend behind the desk. We strolled barefoot along the firm sand where waves lapped the shore, detouring inland when we came across one of the rock piers. Just being that close to the ocean soothed my agitation.

Until Hisako stopped dead in her tracks. She pointed to the shoreline ahead. "What is that?"

I shielded my eyes and squinted. Something large had washed up on shore. A log maybe.

I gasped.

No, it was a person.

Panic washed over me. I stood paralyzed for a second before my lifeguard training kicked in. I sprinted toward the body. As I drew closer, I could tell who it was: Bianca.

Her hair lay tangled about her head like seaweed, matted with sand. Her pale skin was mottled, and her lips were an odd color of blue.

My heart sank right down to my stomach. The ground seemed to tilt beneath my feet. I could hardly breathe. I dropped to my knees beside her. The ties of her halter-top bikini were tangled tight about her neck. My hands trembled as I tried to loosen them.

But as soon as I touched her, I knew. She was dead.

CHAPTER
4

Over and over again, Bianca's voice echoed in my head, "You've inspired me. I think I'll go to the beach." I had challenged her. If it hadn't been for me, she would be alive and well and sunning herself at the pool.

I killed her.

I blinked hard to keep away the tears and fought the bile rising in my throat. It was my fault. My fault. My fault.

I shook my head until my whole body swayed with grief. She couldn't be dead. Not her. Not someone so . . . alive. No! It wasn't right! There had to be something I could do.

I tilted her head back and bent to blow air into her lifeless mouth. Once, twice. Her cold lips had a waxy feel to them. I shook off another rise of nausea and changed position for chest compressions.

"Aphra-*chan*. Stop. It is too late." Hisako's voice was gentle, but it cut into me like the lava rock.

I was not going to accept that. I pumped furiously on Bianca's chest, counting compressions. She did not respond.

"Aphra-*chan*." Hisako touched my shoulder. "It is over."

"No!" The word was more a plea than a denial.

The pressure of Hisako's fingers increased. Gently, but firmly, she pulled me back. Finally, my hands stilled. I realized my face was wet.

"You knew her?" Hisako asked softly.

"Yes. She is . . . *was* a guest at the resort."

"Then we must report it at once."

I straightened. "Yes. Of course." Hisako was right. I was forgetting my responsibility. There was comfort in having something practical to do. I wiped my eyes. "We should get my dad."

"I will go." Hisako bowed. "You stay with the girl."

I drew in a sharp breath. Stay with her? By myself? But of course Hisako was right. We couldn't both go; the surf was already sucking at Bianca's legs. If we left her on the beach unattended, the tide could carry her away. I couldn't let her lie there with a stranger standing beside her, either. I nodded, and Hisako jogged off across the sand.

The whole thing had a bad dream feel about it. I kept hoping I'd wake up and everything would be back the way it was.

But I couldn't pull my eyes from Bianca. She looked so peaceful, like she was just sleeping in the sand. I reached down to brush away a strand of seaweed that hung across her face, and a crab scuttled out from under her matted hair. I screamed and yanked my hand back.

After that, I kept my distance. I was afraid of what else I might find if I got too close. I hugged my knees and stared out at the sea, where a pair of terns spiraled over the whitecaps. Usually their screeches didn't bother me, but that afternoon the shrieking calls sounded eerie and ominous. I shuddered and closed my eyes, as if that could shut out their cries.

At long last I heard voices at the far end of the beach. I pushed to my feet, anxious to share my vigil with the living. That's when I saw him. Adam's dad was standing near the trees, watching me. His eyes flicked past me to the body in the sand and then toward the approaching group. With a half-perceptible nod, he turned and headed back toward villa four.

I watched him disappear into the brush, a strange, cold feeling settling in my stomach. And then my dad was beside me, hugging me, rubbing my arms, studying my face.

"Are you okay?"

I nodded, even though I still felt pretty shaken. The rest of the group ran to join us. Nothing says rush, I suppose, like one dead guest and a handful of live ones you want to keep ignorant of the fact. Dad hadn't wasted any time in gathering his containment team: Darlene, Frank, and the head of security, Junior. No, really. That's his name. Ironically, this guy is about six-four and must weigh three hundred pounds—all of it muscle.

Hisako had stopped just short of where we all stood. Dad gave her a slight bow and mouthed, "Thank you." She inclined her head, turned, and headed back down the beach.

Once she was gone, Junior crouched beside me, balancing his enormous weight on the balls of his feet. "Yup. She wen mahke a'right." "Mahke" was his way of saying dead. Yeah, nothing gets by Junior.

I glanced up. "Where's Mick?"

"Sleeping?" Darlene looked to Junior for confirmation, and then explained. "He was drinking in the lounge all morning, soused as Sinatra. Junior here had to take him back to his villa to sleep it off." I noticed that Darlene had dropped all traces of the island from her accent, something she did whenever she was truly upset. She'd been the one serving him those drinks. I wondered if she was feeling guilty.

Dad's frown deepened. "So that's why she was swimming alone."

And why she had been waiting by the pool . . . before I sent her to the beach to die. I started to cry again. The guilt was mine.

Darlene misunderstood the emotion and draped an arm around me. "We've never had a guest drown before, have we?" She turned to Junior and said in a low voice,

"How could this have happened? The water wasn't even that rough this afternoon."

Frank bent over Bianca's body. "Take a look at this." He pointed to where the ties of her halter-top bikini were wrapped around her neck. "Mebbe she got tumbled by a wave. Wouldn't have taken a big one if she wasn't a strong swimmer. Those strings could'a got caught on something and choked her."

Darlene and Junior nodded gravely.

I shook my head. Something about that scenario didn't feel right. Junior bent close to examine the bruises on Bianca's neck.

I froze, thinking back to the night before when I'd been caught by that wave. The force of the water had pretty much ripped my top off. What it didn't do was wrap the ties around my neck and choke me to death.

And the wave had dumped Adam and me on the sand. Hard sand, not the loose, drier stuff like where Bianca was lying. Her body was too far aground to have been left there by a wave. It was almost as if someone had put her there.

"I don't think she drowned," I said weakly.

Frank looked up. "Right, I think mebee she choked."

Dad cleared his throat. "We'll leave the thinking up to the coroner."

"I hear ya, brah." Junior stood and brushed the sand from his hands. "I get her into the city, fast kine, yeah?"

"Wait!" I pulled away from Darlene. I couldn't shake

the feeling that something wasn't right. They couldn't move Bianca. Not yet. "Shouldn't we leave her where she is until the police—"

Dad cut me off. "Getting the police here could take all afternoon. I am not leaving this girl to bake in the sun. She goes to the coroner."

"But . . ."

Junior looked to Frank. "How soon you can fly?"

"I was just flushing the lines when I got the squawk. Could be a couple hours."

"Where we gonna put her until then?"

Frank took off his Navy cap and ran a hand through his graying hair. "The walk-in?"

Darlene's eyes got big, and she took a step back. He was talking about her walk-in refrigerator in the lounge kitchen. "No way. If any of my staff sees her, they'll flip out. They'd never walk in there again."

Dad waved them quiet. "Lay her in my office. We'll seal it off and crank up the AC. She'll be fine until you can get off the ground." He turned to Darlene. "We'll need a diversion. Send out complimentary tapas and drinks to the villas, and let's be sure everyone is accounted for." He scrubbed his hand over his face. "I suppose I had better go get Mick and sober him up. He'll want to be with her."

It didn't seem fitting to send Bianca off to the city in just her bikini, so while Frank and Junior waited for their diversion, I ran to get a bedsheet. I wrapped her body in the linen as neatly as I could before the guys carried her off on a stretcher.

I followed them to the Plantation House and watched, numb, as they laid her next to the couch in Dad's office and sealed the place up.

Frank mumbled an apology to no one in particular and said he had to get his helicopter ready to fly. Junior plopped onto one of the couches and fanned himself, his round face red and shiny with sweat. "You know, for a little girl, she sure was heavy."

Frank lowered his thick brows and shook his head at that comment, which just made Junior's face turn even redder. He spread his hands and demanded, "What?"

Frank jerked his head in my direction.

Junior rolled his eyes and pantomimed sweeping Frank out the door. Frank left, but Junior hung around the lobby until Darlene stopped by to see how I was doing. The two of them had a low-voiced conversation in the corner of the lobby—as if I couldn't hear every word they were saying. It seems they were worried I'd be freaked out or something if I were left alone with a dead body in the next room. I admit I was a little shaky, but that's not the same thing as freaked, and not from what they thought, either.

They fussed and fretted over what to do with me until their little powwow was interrupted by a loud squawk from the two-way at Junior's waist.

It was Dad. Mick was being, shall we say, a bit hostile about the sobering-up efforts. Dad requested a little muscle as backup.

Darlene sat with me after Junior left, even though I knew she must have had a million things to do.

"I'm fine," I insisted. "I just wish I knew what happened."

She gave me a sad look. "Honey, she drowned. Her top . . ." She raised a hand to her throat.

"Yeah, I know. The strings. But . . . isn't that kind of strange?" I shuddered, thinking back on how cold Bianca's skin had felt when I had tried to loosen those strings—how they were *wrapped* around her neck, not tangled, as Frank hypothesized. She may have been caught, but not by a wave. The ties, her position on the shore . . . it didn't add up.

"What are you saying?"

"Maybe someone . . ."

Darlene pulled back. "Aphra, honey, I know you're upset—"

"It has nothing to do with being upset! There's something off about this whole thing. Her top—"

"Aphra. Don't."

"But it doesn't make—"

Darlene cut me off. "The dead deserve some respect, honey. Let this one go."

I chewed on my thumbnail and looked at Dad's closed

office door. Respect. I'm sure "the dead" would have pre-
ferred to be alive. I wasn't going to let it go. It was my
fault Bianca was gone. If someone had killed her, I had
to find out who it was.

Darlene parked herself in the lobby to work on her
meal lists, but I managed to ignore her. I was busy making lists of my own.

The first thing I had to figure out was who would want
to hurt Bianca? Maybe Mick; they were always fighting,
and he might have believed that, the next time, she really
would leave him. And Bianca did say she'd been waiting
for him. He could have met her at the beach. But both
Darlene and Junior had placed Mick at the lounge at the
time Bianca died. In fact, I had seen him there myself
when Darlene was bandaging my arm.

A chill spread through me as I remembered Adam's
dad, watching from the trees. I tried to shake it off. Lots
of people go to the beach. They just don't stand around
looking over dead bodies and then run off without a
word. Did Mr. Smith have something to do with Bianca's
death? I thought of how Adam would feel if that turned
out to be true, and I felt sick.

What kind of motive could Mr. Smith have? He'd just
gotten to the island. What possible connection could he
have with Bianca? For Adam's sake, I hoped there wasn't
any. But how could I even guess? I didn't know anything
about the Smiths. Not even the basic registration info,

thanks to my dad. And the way he'd been acting lately, I was pretty sure he wouldn't appreciate my asking questions. I was going to have to figure it out on my own. Who were the Smiths? Where were they from?

Wait.

Didn't Adam say he was from Montana? He'd said something about West Broom. Or was that Bloom? It was West something. Was that the name of their town? Could Mr. Smith have known Bianca from before? I had no idea. But it was the only thing I had to go on. Maybe if I found out where West Bloom was, I could find more information on the mysterious Smiths.

I logged on to the computer and quickly Googled: *West Bloom Montana people search*. Point-two-three seconds later I had over a million hits. Nothing on the first page was a perfect match, but I did find a couple of hits for a Bloomfield, Montana. The rest of the page listed hits for a West Bloomfield in Michigan. I scrolled through a couple more pages. The results were similar.

I leaned back in my chair. Adam *had* said Montana, right? Not Michigan? Yes, I remembered his challenging me about knowing where Butte was. Maybe he lived in the west part of Bloomfield in Montana? Is that what he meant?

I pressed my lips together and typed: *Bloomfield Montana white pages*. Maybe I could look them up in the phone book. I opened a site and typed in Smith. All I learned was that there were eighty-eight Smiths in

Bloomfield, but that wasn't much use. And it wouldn't help me figure out what happened to Bianca.

I folded my arms and stared at the screen. I was chasing shadows. It was stupid to think I was going to find out anything sitting in the office. I should just go find Adam. And ask him what? Had his dad killed one of our guests? That would go over well.

Then I thought about something else Adam said at the pool. "Back home" he had gone swimming in lakes. There were lots of lakes in Michigan. Montana had lakes, too, of course, but they were more known for their mountains and their big sky. Michigan had thousands of lakes. And there had been all those hits for West Bloomfield in Michigan. . . .

I rubbed a hand over my face. It was worth a try. I typed in *Adam Smith West Bloomfield Michigan*. The first page was a blog for Adam Smith, a college hockey player. The second linked to an article in the *Detroit Free Press* newspaper.

"How you doing? You look a little stressed."

I about jumped out of the chair. Darlene had finished her paperwork and stood at the counter, watching me intently.

"Oh. Uh, yeah. I'm good."

"So what you working on?"

I hesitated. If she hadn't wanted to hear my theory about how Bianca didn't drown, I wasn't going to lay out my online goose chase for her to scrutinize. "Uh, just homework. Nothing exciting." I clicked on the newspaper link.

"Good for you, but how can you even think straight? My nerves are shot. It was all I could do to post the menu for tomorrow."

I think she kept blathering, but I tuned her out. My eyes were glued to an article by reporter A. Smith from Wednesday's local section of the *Detroit Free Press*. Or, more precisely, my eyes were glued to the picture accompanying the article. It showed a hulk of blackened, twisted metal that had once been a car. Inset near the lower right-hand corner was a family portrait featuring two smiling parents and a good-looking, blue-eyed son. The caption read, "Fiery crash on I-23 claims the lives of local businessman Victor Mulo, art critic Elena Mulo, and West Bloomfield High School senior Seth Mulo."

My hands suddenly felt very cold as I adjusted the resolution of the photo. My head buzzed like I had an entire hive of bees inside my skull.

I had no doubt in my mind; the dead boy and his family were at that very moment residing in villa four.

CHAPTER 5

❝ What's the matter, Aphra?" Darlene edged closer. "You look like you've seen a ghost."

Try three.

I stared at the screen. Adam/Seth smiled at me from the photo.

"Aphra?"

My head snapped up. "Huh?"

"What's wrong? What is that you're—"

Before she could come any closer, I switched off the monitor. "The computer . . . it's starting to give me a headache."

Darlene frowned and stepped behind the desk. She put her hand on my forehead. "Well, no wonder you don't feel good, after all you've been through. You got some aspirin in the office?"

"I dunno." We probably did, but I wasn't thinking about aspirin. I was too busy trying to rearrange what I thought I knew about Adam . . . Seth. The new name was going to take some getting used to, but even harder to wrap my head around was the fact that he and his family were supposed to be dead.

Had the . . . Mulos faked their deaths? There didn't seem to be any alternative. But why? Who were they hiding from? And what did any of that have to do with Bianca?

My stomach tightened. What did my dad know about all this? Looking back on it, he appeared to be hiding the Mulos—putting them in a villa that was not supposed to be inhabited, not keeping records . . .

"Aphra? Did you hear a word I said?"

I jumped up from my chair. "I . . . I need to get some air. Can you watch the desk for a few minutes?"

Darlene blinked. "The desk? But—"

"I'll be right back." I raced from the office before she could object.

Not that I had any idea where I was going. Or what to do with the information I'd just uncovered. But I had to do *something* or I was going to explode. This is what came of getting involved. You end up getting hurt. Seth, if that was even his real name, had lied to me from the beginning. He had said his name was Adam. He'd said he was from Montana. What else had he lied about? I could only surmise that his family had faked their deaths and were on the run from who knew what. Now it didn't seem so far-fetched to think his dad could be a murderer. Or that my dad might be hiding them. It was too much.

I had no one to turn to. Not Darlene. Certainly not my dad. What was I supposed to do now? Spill everything to the authorities? Or should I talk to Seth first and give him a chance to explain? Could I even trust a word he said?

I had to get away. To think. I took a quick glance back at the Plantation House and then slipped into the trees and took off for my beach.

I dropped my shorts, peeled off my shirt, and ran for the water. Holding my breath, I swam along the bottom. I passed through a warm current followed by a downright chilly one. Seemed apropos for the moment, like the ocean couldn't decide what it was going to do either.

When I broke the surface, I struck out swimming, my strokes awkward and jerky—which was about how my brain was working. It wasn't until I found the rhythm in my stroke that I was able to form a clear thought in my head.

What was it Mom used to say? If you can't find the answer to a problem, you need to distance yourself from the situation to see the puzzle more clearly. I couldn't help but wonder what kind of problem my dad and I represented, and why she had felt the need to distance herself from us.

I dove underwater again. I wished I could stay down forever. Then I wouldn't have to deal with moms who leave and dads who can't be trusted. People wouldn't die. Friends wouldn't lie to me.

No, the only thing I could do was to go home. Look for answers. Ask questions. What choice did I have? I swam back to shore.

I knew I was in trouble before I even made it out

of the water, and not from the waves this time. There, standing on the beach, was my dad. He marched down to the water's edge as I came in, his face tight and redder than usual.

"What do you think you're doing?"

I figured it wouldn't be a good move to state the obvious, so I didn't say anything, which turned out to be not such a great move either, judging by the way his lips pulled down at the corners.

"Do you have any idea how worried I was?"

"I told Darlene I was going out."

"To get some *air*, not, not..." He gestured toward the waves. "After everything that's happened today, why would you think this was a good idea?"

"Because I had to get away. *Especially* after everything that's happened today. This is where I come to unwind."

"Not anymore you don't. Not until we get this thing resolved. Now pick up your clothes, and let's go back to the house."

It was pretty clear that Dad didn't know what to do with me. Since I'd never really given him a reason to punish me before, this was new territory for him. As a dad, I mean. As a boss, it was simple for him just to dock my pay or give me the grunt work if I messed up, but in the father/daughter arena, I'd never even talked back to him. Wanted to a few times, but never did. I think I was afraid to.

I could tell he thought he should do *something* about my running off "after all that happened," but he didn't know what. He ended up putting me under house arrest. Not that he came right out and said as much, but he had me work in the office until dinner, and, even then, he asked the staff to deliver the food to the Plantation House instead of our going to the lounge. We ate in silence in the conference room.

I really wasn't hungry, anyway. I kept thinking about Bianca, who at that very moment was being flown to the city by Junior and Frank, and about the Mulos' deception. I picked at my food while fears and questions chased around in my head like a couple of drunken geckos.

I think dad may have noticed my lack of appetite because he eased up a little after dinner and didn't give me any more assignments. He did want me to stay in the lobby, though, no doubt so he could keep a warden's watch on me. I dropped onto the couch with a book, although I didn't see a word on the page.

I have no idea how long I sat there, staring out the window. The knot in my stomach grew tighter and tighter as the sky faded from purple to black and the first stars appeared.

Then I saw movement outside the window. Seth beckoned to me from the shadows. I pretended not to see him and turned back to my book. I coolly flipped the page. Inside, however, I was anything but calm. How could he show his face after the way he'd lied to me? Did he know what his dad had done? Okay, what his dad *allegedly* had done.

I snuck another glance out the window. Again Seth motioned for me to come out. His face looked pleading, anxious. I bit my lip. What if he *had* found out what his dad had . . . allegedly done, and now he needed my help? Could I ignore him?

But he had *lied* to me!

Plus, he and his family could be dangerous if they were involved in something serious enough to make them want to fake their own deaths. I'd be smart to stay clear of him like my dad wanted me to do. Like my dad—who was sneaking around, not telling me the truth, trying to hide the Mulos, treating me like a little kid instead of just telling me what it was all about—wanted me to do . . .

I set aside my book.

Leaning back in the chair, I peered into Dad's office. He was on the phone. Maybe if I just went to see what Seth had to say . . . I rushed to the door and slipped quietly outside.

Seth was waiting by the walk. "Are you okay? My dad said something happened."

I'll bet he did. "I'm good, thanks."

He shuffled his feet. "Do you want to . . . I don't know, go for a walk or something?"

"I can't."

"Oh."

"It's my dad . . ." I gestured vaguely behind me.

"Oh."

The questions inside my head screamed to be asked. Only now, facing Seth, I didn't know how to bring them up without confronting him about his fake death. I wasn't sure if I should spill that without finding out first what was going on. But I couldn't do that by keeping quiet.

"Hey, how did you guys get to the resort last night?"

His brows drew together. "The ... um ... helicopter dropped us on the beach."

I took a step back. The beach? Frank was the only one authorized to bring guests to the resort, and he would never land anywhere but the helipad. I thought back to the night the Mulos had arrived. I *knew* there hadn't been enough time after Hisako's arrival for Frank to have made it to the city and back before the Mulos showed up. "Who brought you?"

He shifted from one foot to the other. "I don't remember the pilot's name."

More lies. An awkward silence stretched between us. Finally, we both spoke at the same time.

"Just wanted to make sure you were all right," he said as I asked, "Are you okay?" We laughed, probably a lot more than the situation warranted.

I searched his face, looking for I don't know what. "Really. Is everything okay? With your family, I mean. Because if you need to talk ..."

Seth never got a chance to answer. Something small and black swooped out of the darkness, aimed directly for my head. I screamed and ducked. Seth was at my side in an instant, protectively wrapping his arms around me.

"What happened?"

I trembled and pushed away, feeling foolish. "It's nothing. A bat. It startled me, is all." Just a bat. The one thing in the world I was most afraid of. Until now.

Seth started to laugh, but then he nudged me and jerked his head toward the office. Through the window, I could see Dad heading toward the door.

"Oh, crap. Go. Go!"

Seth slipped back into the shadows. The sound of his footsteps faded into the shrubbery as the door opened behind me.

"Aphra?"

I turned around, pasting what I hoped was an innocent look on my face. "Yes?"

"Are you all right? What was that noise?"

"There was a bat. . . ."

"What are you doing out here in the first place?"

"I . . . needed some fresh air."

He folded his arms. "I see. And who was that with you?"

"What?"

"I told you, Aphra. I want you to stay away from that boy."

I pressed my lips together. I wanted things, too. I wanted Bianca to be alive. I wanted to see my mom again. I wanted my dad to be straight with me. I opened my mouth to tell him that, but I couldn't make the words come.

I followed him inside, but I wasn't in the mood to pretend-read anymore. "Dad, I'm really tired. I think I'm going to go up to bed now."

He narrowed his eyes. "Bed? Now?"

What was he thinking? That I was going to sneak outside again? I said good night and trudged up to my room. I didn't even turn on the light, but went straight to my window seat and sat staring out over the trees. I hated that my dad and I couldn't trust each other anymore. We may not have had the closest of relationships, but it had worked on some levels. We'd always had a mutual respect. I just wasn't sure it was there anymore.

I must have fallen asleep at the window because when I awoke, I was curled up on the seat, cold and stiff from lying in a weird position all night.

A soft wind blew in a salt water tang from the ocean. It smelled fresh and clean. If only the new day could erase all that had happened the day before.

I showered and dressed and headed down to the lobby, braced for more terse words from my dad. But Dad wasn't there, which was strange; he always began each day promptly at seven o'clock. It was well past eight.

I didn't have time to think too much about it, because just then, Darlene trudged into the lobby, propping up a man in a rumpled navy suit. The collar of his crisp white shirt lay open, and his silk tie hung at a crazy angle. Frank followed close behind with the man's suitcase—a big, blocky thing that appeared to be heavy, the way he was straining with it.

I stared at the procession as they made their way across the room. Another check-in I knew nothing about.

"Aphra, honey, do you know where your dad is?" Darlene sounded irritated. "Frank had to call me to help with Mr. Watson here."

"Watts," the man said.

Darlene gave him a reassuring smile and patted him on the arm like a little child. "No worry, beef curry. We get you settled fast kine, yeah? Guaranz." She lowered her voice and told me, "He got sick on the flight."

Maybe. But even pale and sweating, the man had a threatening air about him that made me want to hide. It was the way he looked at me, with black, veiled eyes . . . like a shark's. Sharp eyes that felt like they were trying to probe my thoughts. Heavy brows hung over those eyes, already disapproving of whatever he might find.

I shuddered and pasted on a courteous smile. "I'm sorry to hear that, Mr. Watson. Let's get you to your room so you can rest."

"Watts." He scowled. "Damian Watts."

I typed in the name and a registration screen came up immediately. It looked like Dad had taken the reservation just a couple of hours before. "Oh. Yes. Here you are. You'll be in villa ten."

"Wait." Mr. Watts pulled away from Darlene and leaned heavily on the desk. He fixed me with those dark eyes. "Mr. Connolly ... is expecting ... me. I need to ... speak to him."

"I'm sorry, Mr. Connolly is assisting another guest at the moment, sir, but I can let him know you're here." I gave him a shaky smile. "Until then, we should get you to your villa so you can lie down."

His thin lips tightened and curved into a frown. "Mr. Connolly—" He swayed, and I thought he was going to pass out right there in the office.

Darlene hurried to prop him up again. "Frank, help me get Mr. Watts out to the cart. You can take him to his room, yeah?"

Mr. Watts shook his head emphatically. "No. I ... need ... to—"

"You need to rest," Darlene said with finality.

I promised to pass along his message to Dad, and Darlene and Frank helped Mr. Watts outside. Once they were gone, I closed out the registration screen as fast as I could. Even having the man's name staring at me gave me the creeps. I didn't know what he wanted with my dad, but whatever it was, I had a sick feeling it wouldn't be good.

Dad showed up around nine that morning with a file folder tucked under his arm. When I asked him where he'd been, he didn't directly answer, but he did ask if Mr. Watts had made it in.

"He's all taken care of. When did we get the reservation? It wasn't on the calendar."

"Late call-in." Dad thumbed the edge of the folder and looked beyond me to the conference room. "Please hold my calls until we're done."

I frowned. "Until who's done?"

"Mr. Watts and I." He paused. "You did show him into the conference room, didn't you?"

"No, he's in his villa. He got sick on the flight. Who is he, anyway? What's this meeting about?"

"Insurance," Dad said too quickly. "It's time to update our policy."

Insurance? Did he think I was a complete idiot? I knew full well our policy was current. Besides, there was no way Watts was an insurance salesman.

"Well, he was looking pretty rough, but I'm sure he'll call when he's conscious."

Dad nodded without saying a word and stepped into his office, taking the file folder with him. I stared after him. Who was Watts, really? And what kind of business could my dad have with a person like that? I watched as he slid the file folder into his desk drawer. One thing was certain: I was going to find out.

Lunchtime came and went. My stomach growled, but I wasn't going to leave the office until I had a look at that file.

Darlene called around one and asked to speak to my

dad. I'm not sure what she had to say, but whatever it was, he hung up frowning. "Aphra, I need you to keep an eye on the office for a moment. If Mr. Watts comes in, tell him I will be right back."

I nodded nonchalantly, watching, hoping, praying that he wouldn't take the file folder with him. He didn't. I waited, blood drumming in my ears, until he cleared the lobby, and then I rushed into his office.

Slowly, quietly, I inched open his desk drawer. The file lay on top of a pile of papers. The label on the tab said simply, SMITH. My breath caught. I *knew* he had to have recorded the information somewhere. But why would he be sharing private guest information with Mr. Watts?

An uneasy feeling coiled in my stomach. Seth's family had gone through a lot of trouble to disappear. Was Watts there to help them or to hunt them down?

I opened the file. Paper-clipped to the inside of the folder were a couple of Polaroid snapshots of the Mulos that had obviously been taken around our resort. Several lined sheets of paper, all filled with my dad's neat handwriting, made up the rest of the file. On the top right-hand corner of the first page was written a notation in red ink: *Watts.*

I wanted to read what the handwritten notes said, but suddenly I heard voices outside the office—my dad and someone else. They seemed to be getting closer. I slapped the file closed and slipped it back where it was.

I probably should have tried to hide or something,

but I couldn't move. The walls seemed to be closing in. Outside the confines of the office, we had a murderer on the loose, an imposter family, and now perhaps a . . . what? What would Watts be? I had to find out, before my dad said the wrong thing and something happened to Seth.

Dad looked puzzled when he returned to his office to find me standing there. I managed to give him a bland hello and reminded him that Darlene had sent over some invoices for his signature. I fished them out of his in-box and handed them to him.

He looked them over. "Any word from Mr. Watts?"

"The insurance guy? No."

He pulled open his drawer to grab a pen and began signing on the dotted lines.

I watched Dad bend over his paperwork, frustration building until I wanted to scream. How could he act like everything was normal? Why couldn't he just talk to me? He could tell me what he knew, and I would tell him what I knew, and maybe we'd be able to make sense of it all. But I didn't have to ask what he thought of the Mulos. That much he had made clear. If I wanted answers, I had to go out and find them myself.

I cleared my throat. "Excuse me, Dad? I'm not feeling very well. Do you need me any more this morning? I think I'd like to lie down."

"No, no. That's fine." He didn't even look up from his papers. "Go rest."

I murmured my thanks and trudged up the stairs, sighing and moaning all the way. In my room, I flopped onto my bed and waited.

Sure enough, Dad showed up at the door within just a few minutes. "Are you sick? Should I get Darlene?" His face was pinched with concern. Made me feel the slightest bit guilty for what I was about to do. But what's fair is fair. If he was lying to me, why should I be honest with him?

"No. It's just . . . you know . . . that time of the month. I get really bad cramps."

His ears turned brick red, and he looked down the hall. I could tell he wanted to escape.

"I think I just need to rest. Is it okay if I skip the office today?"

"Yes. Sure. Fine. I'll, uh . . ." He'd grasped the knob and was already pulling the door shut. "I'll check in on you later."

"Thanks," I called weakly.

I waited until I could hear his footsteps fade away down the stairs and then crossed stealthily to the door. "I'm sorry," I whispered, and depressed the lock.

CHAPTER 6

he trellis looked sturdy enough. A tangle of Kuhio vine clung to the little slats of wood, hot pink flowers long gone in the summer heat. I had no idea if it would hold my weight—I'd never done this sort of thing before.

I threw my uniform clothes on the bed and pulled a pair of worn jeans shorts and a faded OP T-shirt over my swimsuit. Into the pocket of my shorts I tucked the vial of pepper spray my dad kept around for emergencies—just in case I needed protection. Fingers shaking, I tied the laces of my beat-up Pumas and tiptoed back to the window.

My room overlooks the courtyard. It's a great location—it gives me a front-row seat for watching people come and go—but it does make sneaking out a dicey proposition. I watched and waited until I was certain the courtyard was deserted before swinging my leg over the windowsill.

I found a foothold in the latticework and tested my weight against the thin wood. It held. I stepped down with my other foot. So far, so good. I let go of the casement. Not a bright idea. The wood splintered beneath my feet with a sharp crack. In a panic, I grasped at the vines to break my fall, but they pulled away in my hands. I landed smack on my butt, vines snaking down around me.

Actually, it wasn't as bad as I thought it would be. Couldn't breathe for a moment there, but I'd suffered no broken bones. No serious injuries—except to the trellis. I untangled myself from the pile of vines, hoping the rest of the plant was full enough to cover the damage I'd done. Shoving the fallen tendrils behind the trellis, I tried to fluff up the foliage I had crushed at the base. It looked pretty sad but would have to do.

As I turned around, brushing the dirt off my shorts, I noticed Hisako standing near the edge of the courtyard, black eyes alight with amusement. She smiled and bowed to me. My face went hot, and I bowed in return, trying to come up with the Japanese words to explain what the heck I was doing. She placed one finger to her lips and continued on the path as if she had seen nothing out of the ordinary. See, I knew there was a reason I liked her.

I slipped off in the other direction. I had to find out who Watts was and what he was up to before he had that meeting with Dad.

I skirted the main courtyard and headed straight for the maintenance shed. Our grounds crew was working on the other side of the resort that day, but Watts wouldn't know that. I found a uniform shirt hanging on a peg in the shed and slipped it on. It smelled vaguely of old sweat and stale cigarettes, but a dirty shirt was a small price to pay for the truth.

To be clear, I had no idea who the Mulos were running from—or even whether they were running. I didn't know if they were the good guys or if I should be taking Watts straight to them. I didn't know if Seth's dad had anything to do with Bianca's death. All I knew was that I had to get to the bottom of whatever was going on before someone else got hurt.

I grabbed a rake and a pair of canvas gloves and headed to villa ten.

I started raking just up the path from the villa, working my way closer with each stroke. You wouldn't even know anyone had checked into the place, it was that still. No movement in the windows, no lights, nothing. I got bold and worked my way close to the front-room window. I couldn't see a thing for the glare on the glass, though.

Then I heard a voice—no, more like a groan—coming from the veranda. I clutched the rake and snuck around the side of the building.

Watts sat hunched over in a chair, holding a cloth to his forehead. On the table next to him sat a glass of water and a bottle of aspirin. He had removed his tie and undone the top buttons of his shirt, which hung open so that the white scoop of his undershirt showed. When he moved, I caught a glimpse of a brown leather strap cutting into the flesh near his shoulder. My stomach curdled. He was no insurance salesman. The man was wearing a holster.

I retreated backward until I reached the corner of the villa, then spun around and ran all the way back to the maintenance shed.

My hands shook as I undid the buttons of the borrowed shirt. He had a gun. A gun! How had he gotten that past airport security? How had he gotten it past Frank?

I tossed the shirt at the hook and missed. I had just bent to retrieve it when I heard footsteps outside. I froze, my pulse beating in my throat. Had Watts seen me? Followed me here? My eyes darted about the shed. There was no place to hide.

"What are you doing out here?" The voice did not belong to Watts. I'd recognize that fake midwestern accent anywhere. It was Mr. Mulo.

I was about to turn and explain myself when Seth's voice replied, "Nothing. Just walking."

"You can't keep doing this! You know we need to be careful."

"Careful? Dad, there's hardly anyone here! Who's going to see me? I thought we came here so we didn't have to hide."

"No," Victor Mulo said. "We came here *to* hide. You can't be gallivanting around out in the open. We can't risk standing out."

"Then this was a stupid place to come. At least in a big city we could blend in."

"It's only temporary."

"And then what?"

"And then we—" He stopped. "Wait. Did you hear something?"

The voices fell silent.

I held my breath.

"Come. We should get back to the house."

I waited until their footsteps faded away before I dared peek outside the shed. By then Mr. Mulo was at the far end of the path, just starting to turn toward their villa. Seth lagged behind, shoulders hunched, hands dug deep into his pockets. Suddenly he stopped. He turned and looked directly at me. He did not look happy.

My breath caught, and my face flamed hot. I'd been caught spying. Not knowing what else to do, I ducked behind the shed and slipped into the hillside jungle. It's actually a rain forest, if you want to get technical; but with bamboo, banyan, mango, and palms shooting up from the mossy ground, it feels like a jungle. Whatever you call it, it provided a chance to escape while I tried to come up with an explanation to give Seth about why I'd been watching him and his dad.

One of the distinct disadvantages of hanging around in there, though, is that it harbors island mosquitoes. They're about the size of small birds, have tiny needles for noses, and they attack in swarms. Usually I'm careful about dousing myself with repellant before hiking, but in this particular instance I hadn't had the opportunity.

By the time I reached the first ridge, I was covered with itchy, red welts.

Mosquitoes aside, I felt some peace among the ferns and palms. I'd been exploring the hills since the day I arrived on the island, and they had become a refuge to me, just like my beach. Better yet, a few years before I had found a cove tucked back in a little crack of a valley about a mile or so from the property. I liked to think of it as my own private hideaway, which was exactly what I needed at the moment. I didn't know what I would do up there, but at least I had a destination.

In all the time we'd been on the island, I had never seen anyone else at the cove, which isn't much of a surprise because it's easy to miss through the trees, even from the air. I know, because I looked for it last time we flew into the city. I probably wouldn't have seen it at all if I hadn't known it was there. Besides, I doubted any of our guests would expend the effort to climb up that far. You have to hike up to the third ridge, cross a fallen log over a twenty-foot ravine, and slog through an abandoned taro patch. But, oh! Is it ever worth it! A little sliver of paradise, all my own.

On either side of the cove, rocky walls covered in velvet green stretch up to the sky. In the center of the valley, a long, narrow waterfall hangs like a bride's veil and empties into a sapphire pool. The coolest thing of all, though, is the secret cave hidden behind the falls. And no one knew about it but me.

My mom would have appreciated it. We used to go hiking together before Dad and I left for the island, and she was always on the lookout for "little pockets of tranquillity," as she called them.

"Gather peace whenever you find it," she told me once. "Bask in it. Store it up. You never know when you might need it."

Peace was exactly what I needed. Peace and answers. I hoped if I could find the first, I'd be able to figure out the second.

When I reached the pond, I peeled away my shorts and T-shirt and climbed down to the ledge, where I kicked off my Pumas. The rock was warm beneath my feet as I padded to the edge and dived into the chilly water.

Swimming downward, I counted slowly. One-one-thousand, two-one-thousand . . . I could hold my breath for about 239 seconds—pretty good, I think. I once read that pearl divers can stay underwater for three and a half minutes, and I've got them beat. It took just over two minutes to wriggle through the little underwater crevice into the hidden cave, so I had plenty of time to spare.

I popped up to the surface on the other side, gasping for breath. On the rocky bank, I rolled onto my back, staring at the shadowed front wall of the cavern. A long fissure high above me allowed a small amount of light to penetrate the blackness. Crashing down on the other side of the fissure was the waterfall, through which the filtered sunlight cast a jumping, greenish glow across the low ceiling. When I closed my eyes, the light still danced in negative patterns behind my eyelids.

From the upper chamber of the cave came a rustling sound. I went stiff. Bats. I'd always known they lived somewhere deep in the caves, but I had fortunately never run into them. Hearing them from time to time was enough to keep me from exploring beyond the front cavern. I inhaled slow, deep breaths and tried to close my mind to their presence. I couldn't find a tranquil place, though, the events of the past couple of days crowded tranquillity right out of the picture. Bianca was dead, my dad was acting weird, Seth was lying to me, and now we'd added a man with a gun to the mix.

I swatted the water, the splash echoing in a hollow *ploink* throughout the cave. I felt out of control and helpless. More than ever, I needed my mom. She'd always been able to help me talk through my problems until I saw a solution. Who could I talk to now? Darlene? She'd freak out and probably cause more trouble than we were in already. My dad? Not likely. Seth? I didn't know if I could trust him.

My dad sure didn't. Trust him, that is. I thought back on the night the Mulos had arrived—Dad all grins and handshakes until Mr. Mulo's whisper put an end to the party. I wished I knew what he'd said.

Guilt panged at the thought of Dad, despite the fact that I wasn't happy with him. How long before he discovered I was gone? He'd be worried if he saw I wasn't in my room. I should get back. With Watts on the island, time was crucial. If he wanted to talk to Dad about the Mulos, I would just have to beat him to it.

I slid back into the water, took a deep breath, and dived under again. Before going to my dad, I should probably talk to Seth. If I could get him to tell me what was going on, I could go to my dad with crucial information. Maybe then I could convince him to stay clear of Watts.

Wriggling through the tunnel, I mapped out a plan: How I would sneak over to Seth's villa. How I would get his attention. How I would get answers no matter what it took.

Back on the pool side, I glided up to the surface, so fixated on the next piece of the puzzle that I didn't see it standing right in front of me.

"Where did you come from?" Seth stood on the rocks, mouth hanging open, holding my T-shirt in one hand and my shorts in the other. How did he find me? I treaded water, gawking at him.

He returned the gawk. "How did you do that?"

I just shook my head. "Hold on. I'm coming up." I swam to the shore and pulled myself out of the water, all the while trying to come up with a way to ask Seth about the newspaper article. It was a whole lot easier in the cave deciding what had to be done than it was standing in front of Seth and trying to do it. I forced my wet feet into my shoes and climbed the rocks slowly to where he stood.

"No, really," he said. "Where were you? I've been

searching around here for probably ten minutes. I thought maybe you'd drowned or something."

I forced a laugh. "Hey, you should know better than that, after our ocean adventure the other night. I'm indestructible."

"I'll try to remember that."

"How did you get up here anyway? What'd you do, follow me?"

"Well, yeah. I wanted to talk to you. Why did you run away?"

I hesitated. "I was . . . afraid."

He laughed. "Afraid? Of what? I thought you were indestructible."

"I'm not joking."

"Neither am I. See?" He handed me my clothes and spread his hands. "I'm totally harmless."

I looked him square in the eye. "Then tell me your name."

He frowned, hesitating just a fraction too long. "You know my name. It's Adam Smith."

Wrong answer. I turned and started to walk away.

"Aphra, wait."

I waved good-bye with my shirt and kept walking. He ran ahead of me and blocked my path.

"I don't get it. What did I *do?*"

"I know who you are, *Seth.*" I drew out his name and watched the shock register on his face. "I know about you and your dead family, so you can stop pretending."

His jaw dropped. "How . . . how could you know?"

"It doesn't matter. I—"

He grabbed my shoulders and shook me. Hard. "It does matter," he said. "How did you find out?"

I tried to break away, but his fingers dug into my shoulders. Now I really was scared. I fumbled with my shorts, trying to get to the vial of pepper spray in the pocket. It wasn't there. It must have fallen out. I searched the ground. It had to be there somewhere.

Seth lowered his voice, though there was no one around to hear. "Did she tell you?"

"What? Who?"

"Natalie. Did she tell you our names? She promised not to tell anyone our names."

I felt like he'd just slammed me in the stomach. My world spun sideways. I couldn't breathe.

"How," I whispered, "do you know my mom?"

CHAPTER
7

Seth made his face go blank, but not before I saw the "oh, crap" panic pass through his eyes.

"Tell me how you know my mom!"

He shook his head. "I can't."

"Then I can't tell you how I found out your names, either." I twisted out of his grasp and took off down the hill.

"Aphra, wait!"

I could hear him crashing through the brush behind me, and I pushed myself harder. Tears blurred my vision and spilled onto my cheeks. This was a piece of the puzzle I couldn't have seen coming.

Seth caught up with me just past the taro bog. He grabbed my hand and pulled me to a stop. "Aphra, please. I need to know. It's important."

"Yeah? Well, my mom is important to me."

"Please. You don't understand."

"And neither do you."

All of a sudden Seth froze, his eyes darting about the bamboo and ferns.

"What is it?"

He yanked my hand and signaled to me to be quiet.

Then I heard it. From just below the first ridge came a rustling noise. I didn't know of any animals in the area big enough to make that kind of sound, which could mean only one thing. Someone else was in the forest. And obviously Seth didn't want to be seen.

The rustling grew louder, sending a flock of 'i'iwi finches into the air in a burst of scarlet and black. Seth flinched and his grasp on my hand slackened. That was all I needed. I tore away from him and ran down the hill. Seth didn't follow.

I burst through the trees and stumbled to a stop. As if I hadn't had enough surprises for the day, there in the clearing stood my dad and Hisako.

They stared at me like I was some kind of apparition. I stared right back. Out of all of us, Dad recovered first. "Aphra! What's going on?"

I could ask them the same thing.

Hisako bowed. "Jack-*sama,* thank you for showing me the plants of your rain forest. It is a great help for my thesis." She tactfully took her leave.

Without a word, Dad took my arm and steered me down the hill toward home. We'd made it about halfway there before he finally spoke.

"You must be feeling better now." It sounded like an accusation.

Oh, yeah. I was supposed to be sick in my room. "Uh, right. I am. Much better. Thanks."

"You've been swimming?"

I wished I could have come up with something better than, "Um . . . no?"

In the long run it would have been easier just to admit I had been swimming, but I didn't think Dad knew about my cove in the hills, and I wanted to keep it that way.

"I see." Dad folded his arms and walked away. I followed silently. Neither one of us spoke until we had nearly reached the Plantation House.

"I don't know what I'm going to do with you." Dad's voice sounded tired.

"*Do* with me?" What was that supposed to mean?

"Sneaking around. Lying. It's not like you, Aphra."

"I'm not—"

"I told you to stay away from them."

"What are you talking about?"

"Don't play games with me, young lady. You were with that Smith boy, weren't you?"

"No!" Hey, I was telling the truth. His name was not Smith.

"Ever since they came to this island you haven't been yourself. You don't know the first thing about those people, Aphra. I want you to stay away."

I didn't know about them? *He* didn't even know their real names!

"You've left me no choice. You are to stay in your room the rest of the afternoon."

"But—"

"That's final."

"Fine." I turned and stomped up the stairs, making as much noise as I could to let him know I was just as mad as he was. It wasn't until I reached the upstairs landing that I remembered one little hitch. My bedroom door was locked. From the inside.

Now, I don't do this sort of thing all the time, so don't get the wrong idea. I've had to pick a few locks here and there, but nothing illegal, I swear. It's just that in a business like ours, occasions do arise when locks have to be opened, and a key is not always readily available. I learned how to pick locks from our super the first year we were here. We still have the old pin-tumbler types on all the doors, so it really isn't that hard. It just takes time, and I wasn't sure how much I had.

As long as I could hear my dad slamming around downstairs, I knew I was safe, but he could come up to check on me at any moment. I rushed into the bathroom to find something to work the lock. Nothing. Listening for more movement from below, I tiptoed to Dad's bedroom.

His door squeaked as I opened it, and I froze, cursing under my breath. I was supposed to have asked maintenance to oil the hinges weeks ago. The banging downstairs continued, so I slipped inside his room, stealthily crossing to his desk. *Come on, come on.* I rifled through the top drawer until I found two large paper clips. Good enough.

Back out in the hallway, I straightened the paper clips. All I could hear from below was silence. Where was Dad? No time to find out. I tiptoed to my door and dropped to my knees. With a feather touch, I manipulated the paper clips, feeling for the pin stack inside the lock, gently lining them up. I could feel the plug turning. Almost there.

"What are you doing?"

I shot to my feet, palming my improvised tools as I spun around. Dad glowered at me.

"Nothing." I jiggled the handle of my door. *Yes!* I'd done it. I stepped inside and closed the door behind me.

Trembling, I stumbled over to my bed. That was too close. Before the sweat on my palms even dried, Dad cracked open my door.

"You are not to step one foot outside this room for the remainder of the day. Is that clear?"

"Fine."

Beads of sweat stood out on his pale forehead, and he wiped them away with the back of his hand before closing the door. Okay, I knew he was mad, but come on. That was a little much.

Besides, shouldn't I be the one who was angry? I paced back and forth across the room. More pieces of the puzzle were falling into place, and I didn't like what I saw. Thanks to Seth's slipup, I now knew that the Mulos had some connection with my mom. What that connection was, I didn't know, but I could bet my dad did. That night when they came—Papa Mulo probably told Dad about the connection then. That was probably what he had whispered—how he got Dad to let them stay. And it was safe to guess that Dad learned the Mulos were on the run. That would be why he hid them in villa four, and why he thought they were dangerous.

It all began to make sense, except . . . why didn't my dad think he could tell me about it? The Mulos were the first connection we'd had with my mom in four years. Didn't I deserve to know? And what about Bianca? What did any of this have to do with her?

I sank down on the window seat. My chest felt heavy, as if I were buried under a ton of rocks. I stared out at the ocean, realizing, with the kind of clarity that comes with self-pity, that I was utterly and completely alone.

When we first got here, I used to stand at the shore and imagine my mom standing on the other side of the water. I thought it connected us somehow. I was sure one day she would follow the water to where I was. But then the weeks and months and years passed, and I realized that Mom was never coming back to us. I'd never felt so lonely and isolated in my life.

Until now.

Outside, both sea and sky had gone gray. Storm clouds roiled and white caps frothed on the water—a fitting backdrop for my mood.

Just then, I caught sight of my dad as he cut across the lawn and disappeared down one of the many paths into the trees. It was like a sign from God: I wasn't supposed to just sit there and go all emo. For the next few minutes, my dad's office would be empty. At least I could solve one piece of the puzzle. If the Mulos knew my mom, then they likely knew where my mom *was*. That meant that Dad probably knew where she was, too. And I was going to find out.

Forgetting my promise—which, by the way, dealt with stepping one foot outside the room, but said nothing about two—I rushed downstairs, carrying my paper-clip tools just in case.

As I figured it would be, Dad's office door was locked. Crouching in front of the knob, I jiggled the paper clips into the key opening.

"Excuse me, miss?"

I whirled around so fast I nearly fell over. It was Mr. Watts. He looked at me with those cold, appraising eyes, and I nearly swallowed my tongue. Somehow I managed to make myself speak.

"Good afternoon, Mr. Watts. I hope you're feeling better."

"Much, thank you. Is your father in?"

"No, I'm afraid he isn't at the moment."

He frowned. "I need to speak with him. It's a matter of some urgency. Do you know when he'll be back?"

I shook my head. Unfortunately, since I had no idea where Dad had gone off to, I also didn't know when he might return. I glanced nervously at the door. Chances were, it would be any minute.

Watts folded his arms. "I'll wait."

No. That was the one thing he couldn't do. I didn't want him and his gun in the lobby, and I definitely didn't want him talking to my dad. Not yet. I needed more time to sort things out. Besides, if he was there, how was I going to break into the office? "It may be a while."

"Oh? Where is he?"

More important, where was he *not*? Because that's the only place I could send Watts. "He had an emergency to attend to."

"Where?"

"I could have him drop by your villa when he gets back."

He leaned an arm on the counter and glared at me with those cold shark eyes. "I'd like you to tell me where he is."

Suppressing a chill, I put on my most honest expression and gave Mr. Watts directions to the old lava tubes a few miles down the shoreline . . . only you can't walk straight because there's no road, so he had a little workout ahead of him. I hoped it would keep him occupied for a couple of hours and buy me some time to figure out what was going on.

I was afraid those sharp eyes would see right through my deception, but, fortunately, he believed me. "Thank you, miss." He dipped his head. "You've been a great help."

As soon as he was gone, I returned to Dad's office door. It wasn't a difficult lock to pick; I made it through in less than a minute and flipped on the light.

My dad borders on neurotic about his record keeping. He can't not file things away. If he found out where my mom was, I knew beyond the smallest doubt that he would keep a record of some sort. Probably a paper file.

Since I was all too familiar with the filing system, I knew where the information wasn't—in any of the cabinets that lined the far wall of the office. So either the file was in his desk or in the fireproof metal box he kept in the floor under the desk to hold all the important documents like birth certificates, life insurance papers, and stuff. I'd always known the thing was there, but it's not like I've ever had the opportunity to use my passport or anything. I'd never once gotten into the box.

If he felt he needed to keep something hidden from me, it made sense that he'd put it in the firebox, since his desk didn't lock. Just to be sure, I checked the desk anyway, and noticed with disappointment that the file on the Mulos was no longer in the top drawer. As I had suspected, there was also no information on my mom.

Kneeling down behind the desk, I pushed back the rug to uncover the small two-foot-by-two-foot inset in the floor, which housed the firebox. I suppose it was meant to be really secret, but the square lid didn't quite match up with the rest of the floor, so it was completely obvious if anyone cared to look under the rug. I used a letter opener to pry up the lid. It was too easy. Worse, the lock on the metal box inside was a wafer type that was even easier to pick than the door. When we were speaking again, I'd have to have a serious talk with my dad about security.

I rifled through his files until I found a thick manila file folder with the heading NATALIE.

My mom.

My breath caught. I swear I could feel my heart pounding all the way down to my fingertips as I opened the file.

There was no information on her whereabouts. Not that I could see through my tears, anyway. Just dozens of colorful envelopes, all addressed to me. I sorted through them. Each one was postmarked from a different place. The earliest was dated just weeks after Dad and I came to the island, when I was twelve years old. The latest was postmarked a couple of months ago. I tore open one envelope. It was a birthday card. I tore open another envelope and another and another. I could barely breathe. Birthday cards, Christmas cards, "just because" cards covering the past four years. They were all there.

"What do you think you're doing?"

My dad stood at the open door, his hand grasping the doorknob so tightly that his knuckles were white. His ashen face contorted into a mask of anger, the veins standing out like pale crawling worms.

I suddenly found my breath. As if *he* had the right to be angry at *me* after lying to me for all these years! I waved a handful of cards at him. "What is this?"

When he saw what I was holding, his skin took on an even pastier shade than that of his knuckles. "Aphra—"

I slapped the cards on the desk and sprang to my feet, chair banging against the wall behind me. "You told me she was off 'finding' herself! You said you didn't know where she was! You *lied* to me!"

"You don't understand."

"No, I don't. I will *never* understand how you could do this!"

"Now, Aphra, calm down."

"I will *not* calm down!" I snatched up the folder and threw it at him. It didn't quite have the effect I'd hoped for but sort of just wavered in the air before flopping at his feet. He stepped over it and came toward me. I backed away. "She didn't leave us, did she? What did you do, send her away?"

"It was for the best."

"Best for who? All these years I thought she left because she didn't want me! How could you do that to me?"

"I was protecting you."

"From what? What's going on, Dad? Where is she?"

"I don't know."

"I don't believe you!"

"It's true. She moves around."

"Why? What are you not telling me? How does she know the Mulos?"

"The who?"

"The Smiths. Their real name is Mulo. How does she know them? Is that what Mr. Mulo whispered to you the night they came? Is that why you let them stay?"

He mopped his face again.

"Come on, Dad. Out with it."

"You watch your tone with me, young lady." His voice had an edge to it I had never heard before. It only served to make me angrier.

"Or what? You'll restrict me? Take away my privileges? No watching TV or going to the movies? No allowance? Or, wait—why don't you ground me from hanging out with my friends? News flash, Dad: I don't *have* any here. Do you know how it feels to read Cami's e-mails and see what I've been missing, being stuck on the island with you? I haven't seen a movie in four years! We've never once been on a family vacation. And while Cami's off going to the prom, I've never even been on a date. You can't *possibly* make my life any more miserable than you have already."

With that, I stormed out of the office and left him, white-faced and trembling, a defeated droop to his shoulders. He didn't try to stop me, though he may have if he'd known where I was headed. If he wasn't going to tell me what I wanted to know, I'd have to ask someone who would. I didn't stop until I reached villa four.

CHAPTER
8

f Mrs. Mulo was surprised to see me, she didn't show it. She stood at the door like the lady of the manor and invited me inside. I peered into the front room, which was still stripped down to the bare walls.

"I need you to tell me about my mother," I blurted. So much for social graces.

She stepped cordially aside to allow me to enter and then closed the door behind me, shutting out the light. Her face held no expression as she looked me over, sizing me up—as if I'd been the one running around, hiding things. "Why don't we step into the kitchen?"

I followed her down a short, bare hallway. The kitchen was not quite as desolate as the front room, but it wasn't exactly luxurious, either. A table and four chairs sat next to the shuttered window and a stainless steel refrigerator stood in the corner, but the makeshift counter consisted of a length of two-by-four stretched across a couple of sawhorses, and underfoot, the flooring had been pulled up to expose the plywood subfloor. No cabinets hung on the spackled walls.

"Please have a seat," Mrs. Mulo said. "May I offer you something to drink? To eat?"

"No, thank you." I perched uneasily on the edge of

one of the wicker chairs, and she took the seat opposite. I remembered the first night I had seen her in the lobby. I hadn't noticed then that her inquisitive eyes were the same deep blue as Seth's. I tried to ignore the little tug in my chest when I thought of him.

Mrs. Mulo leaned back in her chair. "I'm pleased to see you again, Aphra. Seth has enjoyed visiting with you. He's told us so much about you."

I'll bet, I thought darkly. Still, hearing his name gave me an unexpected thrill. I wanted to blurt, "Oh, really? What did he say?" but I asked instead, "Do you know my mother well?"

She pressed her lips together and folded delicate hands in her lap. At length she answered. "As well as can be expected, I suppose."

"Where is she?"

Her eyes widened for an instant, brows arching, but she hid any further reaction. "I'm sorry. I can't—"

"Does she live in West Bloomfield?"

"I'm afraid I can't tell you that."

"How does she know about your secret? Is she involved?"

Mrs. Mulo reached across the table and took my hand. "Aphra, I can't answer your questions. I'm sorry. Your mother has worked very hard to keep our . . . secret safe. I realize that is not what you came to hear, but please know that digging further could place us all in very real danger—yourself included."

Before I could process what she was saying, she glanced up. "Ah. There you are."

Victor Mulo—the possible murderer—walked into the room. My hands went cold.

"What is this Mata Hari doing in my house?"

I blinked. Was he talking about me?

Mrs. Mulo shot him a look. "Victor, please."

"Please, nothing!" He pointed a finger at me. "You! Knowing the danger our son faces, you lure him up into the hillside—"

"Lure?" I pushed back in my chair. "Is that what he said? Excuse me, but I didn't lure Seth anywhere. He *followed* me. Uninvited, I might add."

"Please. You think I don't know your kind?"

"My *kind?*"

"Victor, please. This is Natalie's daughter!"

He snorted. "Is that supposed to mean something to me? Natalie betrayed us. Her daughter—"

"We don't know that she betrayed anything. We—"

"How else could this girl have known?"

"Stop!" I scraped my chair back and stood. "My mom didn't tell me anything. How could she? She hasn't spoken to me in four years."

Mr. Mulo's brows lowered, and he frowned like he didn't understand what I had just said. I should have stopped then, but I couldn't keep my mouth shut. "Besides, you betrayed *yourself.* You know, yesterday? On the beach?"

He flinched and exchanged a look with Mrs. Mulo. It was all the reaction I needed. In that moment, I had no doubt. He was the one who had killed Bianca. All at once, my bravado crumbled. I couldn't believe this was happening. I'd gotten too close. Would Mr. Mulo feel the need to silence me the way he had Bianca? I backed to the door.

"Look, I won't tell anyone who you are or what you did, but you . . . you can't stay here anymore. Just . . . go!"

With that, I spun to run out the way I had come in. That's when I saw Seth in the hallway, watching me with a sad frown on his face. He looked achingly wonderful in his jeans and T-shirt. Made me want to forget everything that had just happened and stay right there forever. But of course I couldn't do that. I pushed past him and out the front door.

He could have tried to stop me, but he didn't.

Wind whipped my hair into my eyes as I ran aimlessly down the path. Angry tears slid down my cheeks. I swiped them away with the back of my hand. What was I supposed to do now? Everything I had known as truth had crumbled like a house of sand. I had no one to trust, nowhere to go.

"Ho, Aphra, I been looking for you!" Darlene caught my arm. I hadn't even seen her. "Where you been?"

I pushed away. "Not right now. I need to be alone."

She looked me over, no doubt taking in my tears, and shook her head. "No, honey. That is exactly what you don't need." She wrapped an arm firmly around my shoulders and drew me close. I struggled to get away, but she only tightened her grip. "Hey, now. You're gonna hurt my feelings. I'm not such a bad listener, you know." She glanced up at the darkening sky. "Tropical storm moving in. Come on. We can go to my place. I got Häagen-Dazs in my freezer. Chocolate. What d'ya say?"

Well, it wasn't like I had a whole lot of other options. I allowed Darlene to lead me to her place. Like the rest of the staff, she lived in an apartment on the property—except, as a manager, she didn't have to share with anyone. She had a bungalow near the lounge. She'd done it up in an island motif that was about as genuine as her accent, from the tropical leaf-print wallpaper to the fake bird-of-paradise on the bamboo coffee table. True Darlene.

Once she had me settled on the wicker couch with a bowl of mocha almond fudge in my hands, she sat back. "Now tell me," she said. "What's going on?"

I stared out the window to where the wind clinked and moaned through the bamboo chimes hanging from the ceiling of her lanai. "Nothing," I said finally. Nothing I could tell her about, anyway.

"Aphra . . ."

I shoveled a scoop of ice cream into my mouth so I wouldn't have to talk.

Darlene waited. I swallowed my ice cream. She waited some more. I licked my spoon. She cleared her throat. "Aphra. Talk to me. Your father said you were—"

"You've been talking to my dad?"

"He's very concerned about you."

I smacked the bowl down on the table so hard the spoon clattered against the ceramic. "Concerned about me? He ruined my life!"

"He did what he thought was best."

I drew back against the couch cushions. "Wait. You *knew* about it? You knew he was keeping me from my mom?"

"I don't know all the details, but listen—"

"No! Not if you're just going to take his side."

"Come on now. There are no sides. You need to trust your dad."

I snorted. "Trust? Trust is for people who earn it. Four years of lying to your daughter does not cut it."

"He was trying to protect you."

"By letting me believe my mom abandoned me?" My voice grew shrill. "Do you have any idea what it's like to grow up thinking your mother never loved you?"

"Actually, I do. But I didn't have a father who cared enough to try to pick up the pieces. You don't know how lucky you are."

"Oh, yeah. Lucky me. With an absent mom and a dad who can't even be straight with me about why she went away."

Darlene reached for my hand, but I pulled back.

"You've got it all wrong," she said.

"Oh, like you know! You're only taking his side because he's your boss."

"Honey—"

"He made her go away, did you know that? And he never gave me any of the cards she sent. What kind of a father does that? What kind of a sadistic, twisted, rotten, underhanded—"

"Your mother was involved with some dangerous people, Aphra." Darlene's voice rose to match my own. "Your dad hoped that by coming here, she could leave them behind. Start over. But either she couldn't or she wouldn't come. *She* made the choice to stay behind."

"No! I don't believe it."

"His main concern was you, baby girl; you've got to believe that. Your mama loved you, but she could have hurt you. You can see that, can't you?"

"No, I can't."

"I'm so sorry, honey." Her voice was all soft and gushy now. It made me want to hit her.

I just shrugged and looked away.

"And I apologize for this, but there is one more thing I need to speak to you about."

I snorted. "Sure. Why not?"

She cleared her throat. "Your father is a little concerned about your relationship with that Smith boy. You can't be sneaking out with—"

"You don't know anything about Se—Adam! And I

have not been sneaking out!" Well, okay, I actually had, but I hadn't snuck out to meet Seth. It just kind of happened that way.

"Honey, listen to me. Your father says these Smiths are shady characters. Very evasive. I need you to promise you will—"

"Give me a break. If he thinks they're so dangerous, why would he let them stay here in the first place?"

She chewed on her lip. For the first time, she looked doubtful. "I'm sure he—"

Darlene's two-way squawked, and she jumped at the sound. She shot me a "hold on" look, pressed the receiver to her ear. "Speak." Her face fell as she listened. "Yeah? Yeah? No!" She turned from me slightly, cupping a hand over the receiver. "No," she said in a low voice. "Do not move him. I'll be right there."

Darlene signed off, pursing her lips. "Well . . ." She smiled shakily and stood. "There's . . . ah . . . a little problem I need to take care of. You wait for me here, okay?"

I shrugged.

"You get hungry, help yourself to anything in the fridge." She hurried to the door, but paused with her hand on the knob and looked me in the eye. "Promise me you will stay right here."

"Fine."

But promises easily made are easily broken.

• • •

As soon as she disappeared down the path, I began to have second thoughts. It's not that I don't respect Darlene. Generally I do. But it was clear she was going to take my dad's side on everything, so we really didn't have anything else to talk about. I eased out her door and shut it firmly behind me.

The wind had picked up. Dark clouds boiled overhead. Darlene may have been right about the storm, but she was dead wrong about everything else, and I wasn't going to hang around to be lectured.

Up ahead I saw Hisako, long black hair dancing tangos with the wind. Her face was set in a serious frown, and she looked about as lonely as I felt.

She glanced up and saw me watching her. Crap. I cussed under my breath and gave her a polite bow. I would have turned away then, but she gestured to me to wait. I sighed. The last thing I wanted was another forced conversation, but four years of conditioning dies hard. She was a guest. I waited.

"Looks like rain," I said as she neared.

She studied the sky for a moment, then shook her head. "Soon. Not yet." She held out her hand. "Come. Walk with me."

I hesitated. "But the storm . . ."

"I don't mind the little wind." She slipped her hand into the crook of my arm. "Come."

We walked silently, though my mind was anything

but quiet. It was on overload after everything that had happened that day. So much so that I didn't even hear Hisako when she finally spoke to me.

"Aphra-*chan*. Are you here?"

"I'm sorry."

"Do you want to talk?"

I shook my head. I wouldn't know where to start.

Hisako stopped walking and looked me in the eye. "In Japan we have a saying, '*Iwanu ga hana.*' It means to not speak is a flower. But there are times, Aphra-*chan*, when it is not a flower. There are times you must speak the things in your head."

"I'm fine, really."

She regarded me for a moment. "Yes, you are strong. But know this, silence is not always bravery."

"I'll remember that."

She smiled. "I am sure you will." Hisako deftly changed the subject. "All your guests are prepared for the storm, *ne*?"

"Yeah. Everyone should be snug in their villas."

As if on cue, thunder growled overhead. Hisako peered up at the darkened sky. "It will start soon."

"Yeah. I should probably go help bring in the awnings and stack the deck chairs."

"Perhaps the work is already done."

"Probably." I felt a little guilty for not helping prepare for the storm, though I don't know why I should have, after what my dad had done.

She bowed when we reached her villa. "Thank you for the walk, Aphra-*chan*. We will talk again later."

I bowed in return and high-tailed it back toward the Plantation House just as the first fat raindrops fell.

I had nearly made it to the courtyard when Seth stepped out from behind the trees. He took an aggressive stance, chest all puffed out in anger. I drew up short.

"Came to thank you for your compassion and understanding." His lip curled up on one side in what could best be described as a snarl. Water ran in rivulets down his face. He didn't seem to notice. I did. It slicked back his hair and clung to his eyelashes. I wanted to brush the raindrops from his cheeks, his chin, his lips.

"I thought I told your family to go away," I muttered.

"Yeah, well, we'll be on the next charter out, thanks to you."

My heart plummeted. That was what I wanted, right? But if the Mulos went, the answers about my mom went with them. "You can't leave yet. The storm—"

He laughed without humor. "Make up your mind."

I stared up at him, blinking away rain. "Where's my mom, Seth?"

He looked away. "I don't know."

"Don't lie to me! How did you know her? Tell me!"

"I can't."

I stepped back. "Then go ahead and leave. Just go."

"Whatever." He threw a wad of soggy blue fabric at me. "I brought you your shirt."

My face flushed hot. I must have dropped it when we were up at the cove. I threw it back at him. "Drop dead."

He didn't attempt to catch it, but let my shirt fall into the mud.

"Forget it." I tried to push past him, but he grabbed my wrist.

"Aphra, wait."

"Let go of me."

He didn't let go. Instead, he pulled me to him so that we were standing face-to-face—or, in this instance, face-to-chin. I pushed against him, but he held fast. "Listen!"

I glared up at him and he glowered down at me, and when our eyes met . . . well, I can't say exactly what it was. Some sort of chemistry or electricity or something completely unrelated to science zinged between us. A look of surprise crossed Seth's face. His expression softened, and I could have melted right there.

"Aphra, my dad didn't do it."

"What?"

"The girl on the beach. That's what you think, isn't it? That he killed her?"

I swallowed.

"He didn't do it, and he would have tried to save her if he could, Aphra, but it was too late."

"Then . . . why did he just leave?"

Seth shook his head. "We can't be seen. You know that."

Yes, I did know that. What I didn't know was why. "Seth—"

"Aphra!" Darlene's voice cut through the air, driving an immediate wedge between Seth and me. Literally. We must have jumped about three feet apart. She stood at the head of the path, with hands on her hips and murder in her eyes. I watched as those eyes went from me to Seth to my shirt on the ground and back up to me. Her nostrils flared with indignation.

"I've been looking all over for you!"

"I'm sorry, I . . ." My face burned as I bent to retrieve my sodden shirt. "What is it?"

"Something's wrong with your dad," she said. "You had better come with me."

CHAPTER
9

arlene stalked back to the Plantation House without another word. I mumbled good-bye to Seth and ran after her.

"Wait!" I grabbed her hand. "What is it?"

"You promised, Aphra," she said. "I asked you to stay put."

"But the storm. I . . . thought I should go stack the deck chairs and—"

"That's not what it looked like to me." She pulled away and stomped up the stairs onto the lanai.

"Darlene! What's up with my dad?"

The anger cracked as she turned to look at me, and I caught a glimpse of the worry behind it. That scared me even more. She ran a hand through her wet hair. "I don't know what it is for sure. He's having trouble breathing. I think he might be having some kind of an allergic reaction. We've got to get him to the hospital."

"How? The closest one is—"

"I know. That's what I need you for. After Mr. Watts came in, Frank went back to the city to grab Junior. They should be coming in any minute. You need to get up there and tell Frank to wait. I'll get Jack ready. Send

Junior down to help me get your dad to the landing pad. We've got to put him on the return flight to the city."

She didn't have to tell me twice. I threw down my shirt and raced around to the side of the lanai, where the guest cart sat in the middle of a huge puddle of water. I sloshed to the cart, slid onto the seat, and reached down to turn the switch. Nothing. I tried again. Not even a whimper. Battery must've been dead. Probably shorted out from the rain. I took off on foot.

Rain lashed against my face and ran in rivers down the hill toward me. The steps were slick with mud. I stumbled and fell twice, the second time scraping my shin on the sharp corner of one of the stone steps. By the time I limped to the top of the hill, the helicopter was sitting in the middle of the giant painted circle, rotors turning slowly in the wind.

Frank was already unloading boxes from the cargo hold.

"Hey, Frank! Where's Junior?"

He waved to me and shouted over the wind, "Hey, darlin'! Had to leave him back in the city." He looked over my shoulder. "Where's your daddy?"

"That's why I'm here. He's sick! Darlene says he needs to go to the hospital, and she wants you to wait so you can take him back with you."

"No can do." He closed the door and fastened the latches. "This bird's not leavin' the ground till the storm passes. Squall just about took us down comin' 'round the Point. Too dangerous."

"But he needs a doctor!"

"He'll need a mortician if I try to take off in this wind." He opened a small compartment and pulled out a length of rope.

I stepped over the landing skid and ducked to peer under the belly of the chopper, where Frank bent over the securing line, threading it through a mooring anchor. "Listen! Those ropes won't hold if the wind gets as strong as you say. She'll tip right over. You should get back to the city, where you can dock in a nice, safe hangar. And take my dad with you."

He sat back on his heels and frowned at me, shaking his head. "Wish I could, darlin', but I can't. Wouldn't be safe."

"But he needs help!"

"Give me a minute. I finish tyin' her down, and I'm all yours. We'll think of somethin'."

Instinctively I knew I didn't have a minute. "Meet me down there," I shouted, and took off back down the hill.

I'm not ashamed to admit I was scared. As angry as I'd been with Dad, the thought of losing him was too much to bear. I didn't even know what was wrong with him, but judging from the worry I had seen on Darlene's face, whatever it was, it was serious.

I had just made it to the bottom of the hill when I stopped dead in my tracks, my stomach turning to ice.

Mr. Watts stomped up the path toward me, water streaming down his face. He was clearly not happy. "Miss! A word with you!"

"I'm sorry! Emergency!"

I tried to run by him, but he caught up with me and grabbed my arm. Tight. He narrowed his black eyes at me. "No more games. I need to speak to your father."

It took every ounce of control I had to keep from shrieking and running back to Frank. "I'm sorry, Mr. Watts, but my father is very ill. So if you will excuse me—"

"Perhaps I could be of some assistance," he said. His fingers tightened, digging into my skin.

I shivered. No way was that man getting anywhere near my dad. "Mr. Watts, please. Go back inside."

"I haven't *been* inside. I've been hiking all over the property looking for your father, thanks to you. And now you say he's sick—"

"He *is* sick. And I'm busy. Excuse me."

But Watts wouldn't take no for an answer. He followed me to the Plantation House. I planned to run inside and lock the door on him, but Darlene was in the way.

"Hello again, Mr. . . ."

"Watts. I was just telling the girl here that I have some field training, if you'd like me to take a look at Mr. Connolly."

I desperately shook my head no, but Darlene didn't see me. She went limp with relief.

"Oh, thank you." She pumped his hand, pulling him inside. "Jack's not doing too good. Maybe you could help us get him back up to the chopper, yeah?"

"Frank says no," I said. "He says the winds are too strong."

"But—"

"I know. I told him what you said, but he still says he can't fly until the storm passes." I looked beyond her. "Where is he?"

"In his office. Come on."

We tracked mud across the lobby.

My dad lay on the couch shivering, his face even paler than I remembered and shiny with sweat. His lips had a bluish tint to them. I dropped to my knees and grabbed his hand, the clammy skin like death under my fingertips . . . not unlike Bianca's had been. I trembled. "Dad? It's Aphra. Can you hear me?"

His lids fluttered open, and red-rimmed eyes stared at me. A spark of recognition burned behind the dull torpor but quickly faded. His eyes drifted shut once more.

"Dad?" I shook him. "Dad!"

He wheezed in a breath.

Mr. Watts cleared his throat. "Sounds bad. He asthmatic?"

"No," Darlene said. "I thought he was having an allergic reaction or something, but I gave him an epi shot and he's not responding to it."

"How's his pressure?"

"Dropping steadily for the past half hour."

"Shock?"

"Not yet, but I'm worried."

"Can he talk?"

"What do you think?"

I watched them go back and forth like a tennis match. The end conclusion was that Mr. Watts really didn't have any more medical expertise than Darlene. The conversation died down, and he just hovered. Like a vulture. The intense way in which he stared down at my dad looked very predatory. I jumped to my feet.

"Thank you for your help, Mr. Watts."

"Not at all. If you'd like me to stay—"

"That won't be necessary." I steered him from the office.

"If he wakes up . . ."

"Yes, we'll let you know."

Frank appeared in the doorway at that moment, shaking water from his gray hair like a sheepdog. "Where is he?"

I rushed to talk to him. "Dad's resting in his office. Darlene's with him." Lowering my voice, I said, "What happened in the city? Why didn't Junior come back with you?"

Frank leaned close. "Mick took off the minute we landed. Junior went after him. Seems Mr. Rock Star had some possession issues he didn't want to discuss with the authorities. Paperwork got complicated. Thought

Junior woulda been done by the time I went back to get him, but he wasn't, quite. He sent me on ahead and he said he'd follow, but with the storm—"

"Follow? How?"

"The city police want to come have a look-see at the resort."

"Oh, Dad's just going to love that."

Dad. I glanced at his office, and my chest tightened.

"Want me to take a look?" Frank asked.

"Actually, could you make sure this guy gets back to his villa first? He's making me nervous. Just . . . be careful."

"You got it, darlin'."

Frank strode across the lobby and laid a heavy hand on Watts's shoulder. "If you'll come with me . . ."

I ran back into the office where Darlene knelt by the side of the couch. Worry pinched her features as she mopped Dad's face with a cool washcloth. His breathing sounded raspy, and his chest rose and fell in rapid jerky movements.

"Is . . . is he going to be all right?"

"I don't know," she murmured. "I don't know how to help him."

"There has to be something we can do. Call the hospital! Talk to a doctor."

"I called earlier. They said to bring him in."

"We need to call them again. If we can't get him there, they should at least tell us what to do!"

Darlene looked up and nodded at me. I didn't like the

expression on her face. Like she was already mourning his death.

I crossed to the phone and picked up the receiver.

Silence.

The line was dead.

CHAPTER
10

I allowed myself about ten seconds to panic, but that's all. With the phones down, the Internet would be out, too. Our only lines to outside help were gone. But I wasn't about to sit around and act powerless. Not when my dad's life depended on it.

"Think, Darlene!" I insisted. "You are the island guru. What would the locals do in this situation? Isn't there some folk remedy or some kind of herb or . . ." My voice trailed off. Of course. Why hadn't I thought of it before?

"What is it?"

"Hisako! She knows all about plants and herbs and all that. Maybe she could find something to help until we can get Dad to a doctor."

Darlene pursed her lips together and gave a little shrug. I supposed that was her way of saying it couldn't hurt, but anyway, I wasn't waiting for permission. I ran all the way to Hisako's villa, rain plastering my hair to my head and squelching in my shoes. The light in her window shone like a beacon in the proverbial storm. I could see her inside, seated on the floor in a lotus position, facing the wall. Her black hair hung in a single braid down the center of her back. She wore exercise clothes—stretch pants and a tank top. As I got closer, I could see a tattoo decorating one muscular shoulder. I wouldn't have expected that from her—she seemed so demure. I stared at the ornate dragon tattoo and tapped timidly on the glass.

As if she were expecting my company, she rose gracefully to her feet and pulled on a *yukata* robe, tying the sash at her waist as she turned unhurriedly to open the door. When she saw me standing on the stoop, the calm on her face dissolved as she must have read the concern on mine. "Aphra-*chan!* Come in, come in." She stepped aside and motioned for me to enter, but I didn't have time for that.

"I need your help," I shouted, my voice carried away by the wind.

She gripped my hand and leaned closer, worry creasing her delicate brow. "What is it?"

"My dad."

Her grip tightened. "Jack-*sama?*"

"Something's wrong. He can't breathe and he... he ..." The weight of the past couple of days became too much, and I burst into tears.

She grabbed my shoulders and shook me. "Aphra! Tell me what is happening!"

I hesitated. This was all wrong. Hisako was a guest. I shouldn't say too much. I shouldn't—

"Aphra!"

I couldn't help it. One look in her troubled, black eyes, and it all tumbled out. "He . . . looks bad, but we can't get him to a hospital because of the storm, and I . . . I should have noticed something was wrong this afternoon; he was getting all pale and sweaty and everything, but I was too obsessed with the Mulos, and now there's this man looking for them, and I probably should have told him where they were, but I really like Seth and I think that guy might hurt him, and I don't know that I can trust him and—"

"Aphra-*chan!*" She shook me again. "You are making no sense. Please talk slowly. I cannot help if I do not understand."

I told her as much as I could in those urgent minutes, and she listened intently. "I do not believe I have met this Seth. Is he a guest?"

I bobbed my head. "Yes. No. His family is hiding out here. Probably from Mr. Watts, I don't know. That doesn't matter. We need to help my dad!"

Hisako took my hand. "We will, Aphra-*chan,* but we must also stop this man," she said. "Do you think he is dangerous?"

I nodded.

Her mouth set in a straight line. "Then you must see to this Mr. Watts," she said. "I will gather medicines and go to Jack."

"Thank you. Thank you!" I bowed deeply.

"I will meet you there." She gave me a quick bow and then stepped inside to change her clothes.

I left her villa, mind churning. She said I should deal

with Mr. Watts, but couldn't that wait? First I wanted to make sure my dad was okay. I started up the path toward the Plantation House, but I couldn't shake the image of Mr. Watts's cold smile from my head. My gut told me he was dangerous. I could feel it.

But were the Mulos dangerous, too? Seth's face swam before my eyes, and for one delicious moment, I could feel his arms around me. Danger did not fit my image of him at all, but was I thinking clearly?

At the head of the path, I hesitated. I didn't have time to sort out who was good and who was bad. And if I chose wrong, how could I undo it?

The branch of a coral tree blew into my path, and I kicked it out of the way.

Then I had an idea.

When Mr. Watts answered the door, he blinked at me, surprised. "What is it? Your dad doing better?"

"Uh, soon I hope. Thanks. I, um . . ." I raised the domed silver tray I held in my hands. "The kitchen will be closed until further notice because of the storm, so the chef sent me down with a complimentary supper."

"In this weather?"

"Yeah. You're my last delivery, and then I can go home. May I come in and set this down?"

He stood back, holding the door open with one arm. I stepped into his lair. My hands were shaking so bad that the silverware on the tray rattled. I slipped off my muddy shoes and padded barefoot into the entry, trailing water in my wake. "Where would you like it?"

"There is fine." He pointed to a small table near the front window.

I set the tray down gently and raised the lid with a flourish. I have to say that the salad was artfully arranged: cucumber, tomato, and carrot curls atop butterhead and romaine, set off with a sprinkling of bright red coral seeds. Not a bad job, given my haste.

Next to the salad plate sat a basket of rolls with butter, and a small cruet of dressing, specially doctored by yours truly. Even if he ate it all it wouldn't do permanent damage, but the amount of salvia leaves I used in conjunction with the coral should knock him out for a good couple of hours. And just in case he wasn't a salad fan, I had brewed a small pot of jasmine tea, careful to include kava root in the blend.

He stood uncertainly and then bent to sniff the aroma of the fresh-baked rolls. Well, not exactly fresh baked since the kitchen truly was closed, but I had zapped them in the microwave before tucking them into the basket. As he reached forward to grab a roll, I noticed a bulge under his shirt, just below his left arm. The gun. I swallowed hard and backed to the door. *"Bon appétit."* With a hasty bow, I ducked out the door and closed it behind me.

I couldn't get out of there fast enough. Still, as I reached the top of the path, I ducked behind a tree and looked back toward the villa. Through the bucking branches, I could see Mr. Watts pull a chair up to the table and unfold the napkin onto his lap. He ate like a starved man, barely pausing between bites to take a sip of tea. Rain pelted me with increasing fury, but I hugged my arms and waited. I wanted to get back to the Plantation House, but not before I made sure the job was done.

It didn't take long. Before he even completed his meal, Watts yawned and stretched like a satiated cat. Standing unsteadily, he staggered to the couch, where he flopped down for what I hoped would be a very long nap.

Hisako hadn't gotten there before I returned to the Plantation House. Darlene stood at the door to the office, wringing her hands. "Well?"

"She's coming. She had to gather some things together."

"Does she know what to do, then?"

"I hope so. How's Dad doing?"

She didn't answer with words, but the look on her face spoke volumes. My heart fell. I stood in the doorway with her, dripping water on the floor and feeling very small. On the office couch, Dad lay on his back, one arm thrown over his eyes. His face was gray as a corpse. Small gasps escaped his lips as he struggled for each shallow breath.

"Daddy," I whispered, "please don't leave me."

With uncanny timing, the front door blew open with a loud crash. I jumped and whirled around to see Mr. Mulo framed by the doorway, backlit by the raging storm, his raincoat whipping in the wind. He strode into the lobby carrying a black bag. Mrs. Mulo and Seth followed close behind.

"Where is he?" Seth asked.

Mrs. Mulo rushed to the office and peered inside. "Victor! Come quick!"

He pushed past me and bent over my dad.

Elena Mulo touched her husband's arm. "You must help him. He looks very bad."

He threw an anxious glance at Darlene and me.

"Victor." Mrs. Mulo's voice grew sharp. "Aphra knows already, and Miss . . ." She looked to Darlene with raised eyebrows.

"Darlene," I supplied.

"Miss Darlene will not utter a word of what she sees here, will you?"

Darlene shook her head dumbly, obviously confused. As was I. What was she talking about?

Mr. Mulo dropped to one knee beside the couch and placed a knowing hand on my father's forehead. He opened his black bag and pulled out a wooden tongue depressor and a silver flashlight with a narrow black tip—the kind they use for physical exams in the doctor's office.

He glanced up impatiently. "How long has he been like this?"

I shook my head, still bewildered. "I . . . I'm not sure."

"He passed out about two hours ago," Darlene offered. "I gave him an epi shot."

Mr. Mulo shook his head. "This does not appear to be an allergic reaction."

"I don't understand," Darlene said.

"Victor was a doctor . . . before," Mrs. Mulo whispered, as if that explained everything. She peeled off her raincoat and dumped it on the counter and then hurried to assist her husband.

"I don't have the right equipment, Elena," Dr. Mulo said. That title would take some getting used to. What else didn't I know about Seth's family? Whatever it might be, I did feel better watching Dr. Mulo poke and prod my dad. The man obviously knew what he was doing.

"I know you wanted us to leave the island, but they can help. I had to tell them." Seth's voice rolled over me like a summer zephyr, warming me despite my sodden clothes.

"Thanks," I murmured.

Darlene planted her hands on her hips. "Anyone mind telling me what is going on?"

I waited for Seth to explain, but he said nothing. "Their name is not really Smith," I said simply, and left it at that.

Dr. Mulo gestured to Darlene to come closer. I followed.

"His airway is compromised. If this continues, we may need to intervene."

"Intervene?"

"Tracheotomy." He scribbled notes on a small piece of

paper and handed it to her. "Here is a list of things I will need in order to be prepared. We shall hope it doesn't come to that."

"Hisako will bring us something," I said hopefully. "She said she would come."

"Who is this Hisako?" Dr. Mulo looked alarmed. "We cannot be exposed to anyone else."

I didn't have the heart to tell him that Hisako already knew all about them. "She'll be discreet."

"What is it she is bringing?"

"I'm not sure. Some kind of herbs or something. She's a botanist. She's looking for something to help."

He grunted. "She can give you these herbs without coming in here, can she not?"

"I . . . I guess so."

"Go see what she has and bring it back directly." Then, turning to Darlene, "You gather these items, just in case."

I ran to the door, and Seth followed. "I'm coming with you!"

I wasn't about to argue.

The storm nearly whipped the door from its hinges when I opened it. It probably would have knocked me right over if I hadn't been holding on to the door frame. Seth took my hand, and we struggled together against the wind, heads ducked to keep the rain from stinging our eyes. I led him to Hisako's villa. Her windows were dark, but I pounded on her door anyway and called her name.

"She must still be out gathering the plants," I yelled. "We should look for her."

"Where?"

"I'm not sure. She'd probably be able to find more variety up there." I pointed to the jungle behind the property.

"What are we going to do? Comb the entire hillside? We'd never find her."

"We've got to try!"

He shook his head. "Aphra, it's getting dangerous out here. We can hardly see as it is."

"Seth, I need her. For my dad."

He nodded without a word and took my hand again. We followed the trail that led to the far south corner of the property. Bits of sand and twigs flew through the air, stinging my skin like needles. A branch of a tree shot out of the darkness like a javelin. It missed Seth's head by inches. It was stupid being out in that weather, but I didn't know what else to do.

As we rounded the corner of the shuttered lounge building I saw a figure sprawled on the ground. Even in the darkness, I could tell it was too big to be Hisako. Stumbling toward the body, I swiped water from my eyes. "Frank!" I dropped into the mud beside him and shook his shoulder. "Are you all right? Frank, talk to me!" I slipped my hand under his head to lift it from the water, and my fingers touched a huge knot at the back of his skull.

"He's been hit on the head!"

"Something in the wind, maybe?"

"Probably." Or . . . maybe some*one*. But who? Watts was dead asleep in his villa. My stomach seemed to fold in on itself. What if Watts wasn't working alone? If the Mulos had managed to get on the island without Frank, what would've stopped someone else from dropping in? That person could be prowling about the resort right now! He could have been the one to kill Bianca. The Mulos could be in more danger than I had thought.

"Seth! I need you to get Frank back to the office. Have your dad check him for a possible concussion. I've got to go see something."

"I'm not leaving you out here alone!"

"I'll be right behind you. I just need to do this." I took off before he had a chance to protest and ran as fast as the wind and the mud would allow, all the way to villa ten.

Just like Hisako's had been, Watts's windows were completely dark. A tickle of fear caught in my throat. If Mr. Watts was still sleeping as I'd left him, who had turned off the lights? I crept to the front window and pressed my face against the glass to peer inside. A flash of lightning lit the front room where I had seen Mr. Watts drop onto the couch.

As I had feared, the couch, the room, and all that I could see was empty.

CHAPTER
11

anic lashed at me like the wind and the rain. How could he have eaten everything I gave him and not have it affect him at all? Maybe he had help. Maybe they knew I had been trying to drug him, which meant that I could have placed us all in more danger. Someone had already attacked Frank. My stomach dropped. Hisako was out there looking for plants. What if they went after her, too? I had to get help.

I wheeled around and tore back to the Plantation House. Slamming through the doors, I ran smack into Seth. He grabbed me to keep me from falling.

"What is it? What's wrong?"

Everything. I clung to his arms and wished I could die right there so that I wouldn't have to face him and tell him how I had betrayed his family. I should have told the Mulos the moment I realized Watts had come looking for them. Should have warned them that someone else might be on the island. Now they were trapped. At that point, I didn't even care who the Mulos really were or what they may have done. All I could go on was the feeling of dread gnawing at my chest.

"Seth, you and your family are in danger."

He tensed and held me from him. "What are you talking about?"

I looked away, unable to let him see the guilt written on my face. "There's a man. Here on the island. Looking for you—for your family."

Seth's eyes slid to the office, where his parents were busy attending to the needs of my father. I felt like such slime. "I didn't tell him anything." My voice sounded whiny. Pleading. Like I was trying to convince myself as well as him that I had done all I could to protect them. It just wasn't true. "Seth, he may not be alone. Whoever hurt Frank could be coming after you next."

Seth's grip tightened, pinching the skin on my arms. "Mom! Dad!"

Elena Mulo was the first to respond. She appeared at the office door, clearly shaken by the urgency in Seth's voice. "What is it?" Dr. Mulo joined her, his face showing the strain of the past hour.

"They found us."

Dr. Mulo looked stricken. "How can it be possible?"

Mrs. Mulo didn't say a word, but shook her head, the color draining from her face.

"A man came today," I said. "Asking about you."

Darlene came down the stairs at that moment. "Frank is resting comfortably. I gave him the icepack. . . ." Her voice trailed off. "What is it?"

The lights flickered, and then everything went dark.

Mrs. Mulo gasped. Darlene tried to reassure her. "The storm."

I knew better. The resort's emergency generator would have kicked in the instant power was interrupted. This was no accident. First the phones and now the power.

"Lock the doors." I pulled away from Seth. "Hurry!"

I have to give Darlene credit. She didn't even ask why, but rushed to the front doors and drew the bolt. I ran to the back entry and did the same. I even checked the French doors that led out to the lanai, although I knew that, with its flimsy lock, if someone wanted in, all it would take was one well-placed kick and we were done for.

"Victor . . ." Elena Mulo's voice cut through the shadows, tight as an overwound piano wire.

Darlene looked from one to the other. "Someone tell me this instant what is going on!"

"Everyone just calm down," ordered Dr. Mulo. "Hysteria will do us no good. Aphra, you will tell us what happened. In the back room. I need to monitor your father."

Silently, we filed into the office. The only light came from a battery-operated clock on the wall. It washed the room with an eerie yellow glow.

Dr. Mulo squatted near the couch next to my dad, and Mrs. Mulo sank onto the rolling chair behind the desk. Dad's breathing still sounded labored, but not as raspy as earlier. Seth edged into the crowded office beside me. I wanted to draw comfort from his closeness, but my guilt wouldn't let me.

"Tell me." Darlene folded her arms in the tough-girl stance that was supposed to show she wasn't scared. She didn't fool me for a minute.

I repeated what I had told Seth. "Frank's the one who took Watts to his villa," I said. "Maybe he was asking too many questions, I don't know, but I think someone hit Frank over the head and left him out in the storm."

"Why would anyone do that?"

"They're looking for us." Mrs. Mulo's voice was so soft that I could hardly hear her for the wind outside. She held up her hand as Dr. Mulo began to protest. "We may as well tell them the entire truth, Victor. They could be in danger because of us."

His shoulders drooped. "We never thought it would come to this. We were certain no one would find us here."

"Even the agency does not know where we are," Mrs. Mulo added.

"Agency?"

"The bureaucrats nearly got us killed—although we may not have done much better ourselves."

"Why would anyone want to kill you?" From what I could see of Darlene's face in the dark, she was at once captivated and horrified.

"It was my fault," Elena Mulo said. "I crossed the wrong man, and now he's after us. Our only option, if we wanted to live, was to not exist anymore. Victor arranged the accident to make it appear as if we were dead. We thought we had forgotten nothing—"

"But it did not take long for Aphra to see through our guise," said Dr. Mulo. "We apparently did not cover our tracks as well as we thought."

Darlene frowned at me, no doubt peeved that I had kept this secret from her. I frowned back, just as confused as she was.

"Seth was our conscientious objector," Dr. Mulo continued. "He warned us that this would not work. He said that we would only endanger those who tried to help us. I am sorry to say we did not listen. He was right. We should not have come."

I stared at Seth's parents, trying to process what they were saying. If Mrs. Mulo had witnessed a crime or something like that, they had probably been in the Witness Protection Program.

Dr. Mulo looked at me with sad eyes. "I'm afraid your friend on the beach may have died because of our folly. I had feared as much when I saw her—that her death may be some kind of warning—and if what you say is true . . ." His voice cracked. "I am so very sorry."

Seth shifted beside me, and his arm brushed mine. I flinched. There was plenty of blame to go around. I may not have been able to stop Bianca's killer, but I could have warned Seth's family—if I hadn't suspected his dad to be a cold-blooded killer.

A change in Dad's breathing brought an end to the self-recrimination. He gasped and gurgled as if he were being strangled.

Dr. Mulo checked my dad's throat. "The swelling has gotten worse." He looked to Darlene. "You have the items I asked for?"

She nodded, looking unsure. "Do you have to cut him? Isn't there anything else? The herbs?"

My stomach sank. In my panic, I had forgotten about Hisako. She was out there alone. "I . . . I didn't find—"

"There is no time to wait." Dr. Mulo rolled up his sleeves. "I will need light."

"I'll get the flashlights!"

Seth followed me to the registration desk, where I grabbed a halogen flashlight. "Give this to him." I handed it off. "There's another big one in the utility closet."

The lobby was darker than the caves at midnight, except for the occasional strobe of lightning. I felt my way to the utility closet and fumbled in the blackness for the lantern flashlight. I grasped the handle and turned around just as a tremendous flash bathed the lobby and the surrounding lanai in brilliant white light. In that instant, I thought I saw a figure duck behind one of the pillars. I swallowed a scream, nearly dropping the lantern. Fingers trembling, I switched it on, shining the powerful light along the length of the lanai. Nothing. Still, my heart was doing ninety. There had been someone out there, I was sure of it.

"Aphra! The light!"

I ran back to the office. Darlene directed the beam of the smaller flashlight to where Seth was pouring the alcohol over his father's hands. The excess dribbled into a small metal bowl on the desk. Dad sounded even worse by now. His whole body arched with the strain of drawing each new breath. He was suffocating to death while someone lurked outside to kill the only person on the island who could give my dad a chance at life.

I handed the flashlight to Darlene. "Here, hold this. I . . . I think there's another one upstairs." I rushed out of the office, snagging Mrs. Mulo's raincoat on my way past the front desk.

No matter what the Mulos' story was, one thing I knew for sure: I should have given them a fighting chance. I had placed them in danger with my silence. The only way I could think of to set things right was to protect Seth's family and ensure that Dr. Mulo had time to perform the procedure on my dad. It was up to me to get that assassin away from the Plantation House.

In the darkness of my room, I yanked out dresser drawers, dumping them on my bed and pawing through my clothes until I found what I needed—long black pants and a white T-shirt. I wiggled into them and fumbled in my desk drawer for the flashlight and a pair of scissors.

In the bathroom, I locked the door and set the flashlight on the counter. The yellow beam of light cast weird shadows on the walls and made my face look alien in the mirror. I closed my eyes, lifted a handful of hair, and cut it off. It didn't matter if it was perfect, just so long as no one saw me up close. If I was lucky, that wouldn't happen. Before long, dark hair carpeted the sink, the counter, and the bathroom floor. I slipped on Mrs. Mulo's raincoat and stared at my altered reflection in the mirror.

It would have to do.

Lightning strobed through the windows as I tiptoed down the back stairs. A clap of thunder shook the house. I took that opportunity to slip out into the storm.

I am Elena Mulo. Come and get me.

The wind whipped her coat around my legs. Rain pelted me like liquid marbles. I ducked my head and ran toward the front of the house, where I had seen the man hiding. My idea was to get his attention and draw him into the jungle, where I had the advantage. I knew every inch of the hillside, and he did not. If I managed to lose him up there, he could wander for hours before finding his way back down—just enough time for Dr. Mulo to perform his magic.

Only the killer didn't follow the script.

Before I had even rounded the corner, a bullet zipped past my ear. I wasn't sure what it was until it slammed into the pillar next to me, sending splinters of wood flying. I screamed and dropped to the ground. Sodden blades of grass poked my cheek, and water soaked through my clothes.

This wasn't exactly what I had planned. I hugged

the ground, frozen with fear. A spray of grass and mud jumped up not six inches from my face. I choked back a scream. It wasn't going to do me any good to lie there like a fish on a platter. He could finish me off, and then what? My dad would die. I had to give Dr. Mulo more time.

I pushed myself up from the ground and ran in a zig-zag to the tree line, hoping he would follow—only not too close.

Sure enough, his footsteps crashed through the undergrowth behind me. He was coming.

I climbed harder, but the heavy rain weighted my clothes and stung my eyes. I slipped and stumbled up the hill, decomposing leaves slick and wet beneath my feet. My thighs burned. My chest grew hot and tight. I wanted to stop and catch my breath, but I could hear him behind me.

Close. So close.

Inches from my head, a banana leaf jumped and ripped apart. Half a breath later, a bullet splintered the palm trunk beside me. I dropped to the ground once more, the sound of my scream caught in my throat. I swore I could feel the vibration of his footsteps coming nearer.

I held my breath, wishing and praying. . . . I wished I could tell Seth how sorry I was. I wished I could have protected Bianca. I prayed for the chance to see my mom one more time before I died.

The footsteps hesitated and then stilled. I squeezed my eyes shut. *Please, oh please, oh please.*

He headed off in the other direction.

I could have cried with relief . . . until I realized that he was heading back down the hill. No! I jumped up. He couldn't go back to the Plantation House.

The sound must have drawn his attention, because the course of the footsteps changed once again. I spun and scrambled through the tangle of trees and vines, the crack of branches sharp and clear behind me. Mud sucked at my feet as I struggled up the hill. Mrs. Mulo's coat kept getting caught on branches, slowing me down. I should just dump it right here, I thought. I should—

The sleeve of the coat jerked as if someone had tugged on it. Something hot zipped over my skin. I clamped my hand over the burn, and ducked behind a jambu tree. I couldn't breathe. The earth tilted and my head buzzed as I looked down at the small hole in the fabric of Mrs. Mulo's coat. The bullet had just barely missed my flesh.

Adrenaline fueled by cold, raw fear spurred me on. I broke from the tree and raced through the shadows to a stand of bamboo. Wind snaked through the narrow trunks with a haunted, moaning sound that chilled me even more than the rain. I didn't have to look back to know he was close behind me. My back tingled with the kind of dread you feel when you know someone could jump out and grab you at any second.

With the weight of the coat and the way it kept snagging on branches, I tired much quicker than I would have otherwise. Still, as much as I wanted to, I didn't dare take it off. Not yet. I had to preserve the illusion a little longer. My thigh muscles burned as I climbed up the hill. My breath came in tearing rasps, and my side ached as if someone had stabbed me with a hot poker. Finally the ground leveled off and I could breathe a little easier, though I didn't dare slow my steps. I wasn't going to give the assassin another chance to take aim. Ducking in and out of the trees, I led him farther up the mountain.

He was gaining on me. I would never lose him. Unless . . . I changed direction and scrambled under low-hanging branches toward my hidden cove.

The rain began to taper off by the time I reached the ravine. I thanked the gods; the old log was dangerous enough to cross on the best of days. Water in my eyes wouldn't do much to improve the situation.

I hesitated at the tree line. Crossing the log, I would be completely exposed with nowhere to go but down. Still, it was my only chance. I took a deep breath and went for it.

The log shifted after I had taken several steps—the ground beneath it no doubt eroding in the rivulets of water that continued to flow down the hill. I froze. My chest felt like it was clamped in a vise. If the log fell . . . I glanced down and was instantly seized by a grip of vertigo. Only the knowledge that a killer was close on my trail kept me going. I took another tentative step. The log held.

A shot exploded behind me. I screamed and lost my footing. My arms windmilled in the air before I fell. I reached out for the log and slammed against it with a thud.

I hugged the log, fingers gripping the rough bark, feet treading empty air. I could hear the killer and twisted around to see a black figure moving among the shadows. Out there on the log I was as good as dead, which wouldn't do my dad or the Mulos any good. And I'd never get the chance to find my mom. That thought gave me the surge of strength I needed to swing one leg high enough to hook it over the log. Grunting from the effort, I pulled myself up. I shimmied the rest of the way along the log until I reached the muddy ledge on the far side of the ravine. Solid ground! I rolled onto my back. I never wanted to move again.

Of course, I didn't have much choice. He was coming, and I couldn't leave the log in place for him to cross. I pushed myself into a sitting position, braced my back against some rocks, and pushed my feet against the end of the log until it gave way and tumbled down into the ravine. The rotted wood smashed into pieces at the bottom. I let out a breath. At least he wouldn't be able to reach me.

My relief didn't last long; a bullet ricocheted off the rock next to my head. I screamed and rolled to the side, scrabbling in the mud to reach the safety of the trees. In the shadows, I stood shakily and turned back just in time to see my pursuer running at full speed toward the ravine.

Time slowed, and I watched frame by frame as he flew through the air, arms and legs working for more distance. His feet hit the edge but slid backward in the mud. I was sure he was a goner, but at the last moment, he pitched forward onto his stomach and grabbed handfuls of weeds before the momentum could drag him down.

I didn't wait to see more, but spun around and ran, the focus of my world narrowing to one objective: staying alive.

CHAPTER 12

The weird thing about being terrified is that it heightens your senses. I would have thought that your mind would shut down and you'd obsess about what was making you scared, but that's not how it happened. Everything around me came into sharp focus, from the spongy texture of the jungle floor to the clean rain scent mixed with the earthy smell of humus. The hum of insects and tree frogs finding their voices after the storm seemed to be calling out to me. Run. Hide. Run. Hide.

I became acutely aware of the noise I made smashing through the undergrowth and winced at every footfall, knowing that he must be hearing it, too. I could hear him. Not clearly, but enough to know he was back there. Coming. My aim was to put enough distance between us that I could slip into the cove without leaving a trace.

Thing was, between my sanctuary and me lay the marshy old taro patch. On the best of days it's a challenge to slog through. After the rains, it was even worse. Wild and overgrown and about the width of a football field, I knew it was going to slow me down, but there was nothing I could do about it. I slipped into the bog, hip-deep in water and sludge that sucked and pulled at my legs as if it wanted to root me to the hill forever.

I hadn't made it far before I heard a crack in the jungle behind me. I dropped to my knees so that the muck closed around my chest and the huge, arrow-shaped leaves formed a canopy over my head. At least that was something to be grateful for; I'd be well hidden while I made my escape. I slid through the putrid water like a snake, navigating between the rows of taro plants.

Another rustling came from the undergrowth, much closer than before. I froze. Sheltered under the shadow of the clouded sky and the protective leaves of the taro, I considered the merits of staying right where I was. Except for one thing. The stagnant waters of the taro patch were the perfect breeding ground for mosquitoes. The rain had stopped now, and the mosquitoes had resumed their hunt for blood. There I sat—a living, breathing smorgasbord. They were all over me. I tried my best to wave them away, but there were too many of them. One landed on my face and sunk its proboscis into my skin. I flinched and reflexively swatted my cheek. Not a smart move. The noise apparently caught the killer's attention because the rustling behind me became louder, more distinct. Even though I couldn't see him, I knew he would be looking over the taro field now. It would be only a matter of time before he found me.

I eased toward the bank, gauging the distance between the end of the bog and the line of trees beyond. I had enough of a head start that I could probably lose him in the jungle. The questions were, how well he could aim in the dark, and was I willing to take the chance?

A splash at the opposite end of the field made the decision for me. He wasn't going to wait until I showed myself; he was coming to find me. I couldn't let him do that.

I slogged to the edge of the bog and tried to climb out, but the banks had turned to mud and kept coming away in handfuls. Behind me, I could hear him sloshing through the muck, tearing the plants out of his way.

In desperation, I dived at the bank, throwing myself as high aground as I could. When I was able to pull myself up, I crouched and ran for the trees.

I didn't stop until I reached the clearing that surrounded my hidden pool. In the darkness it looked like a different place. Instead of the serene, magical escape I found during the day, the shadows were menacing, the lulling sound of the waterfall now like the roar of a feral beast.

The plan was simple enough: to swim to my cave and hide there for as long as it took for the assassin to go away. Of course, life seldom works out the way you plan.

I ran toward the ledge, but my foot hit something and I stumbled. Whatever it was went skittering across the rocks. I squinted through the dark. My vial! I reached for it, but it tumbled over the ledge and clattered to the rocks below.

Those extra moments cost me a clean escape. The unmistakable sound of movement among the trees sent new tremors of fear through my body. I spun around, looking for someplace to hide. I couldn't jump into the pool now. The splash would alert him that I was here. I rushed into the shadows of the huge stones near the cliff wall just as he emerged from the jungle. Holding my breath, I watched as he scanned the clearing. In the darkness, I could make out only his shape as he crept like an animal on the prowl, light-footed and feline. He paused at the ledge and surveyed the empty water below before climbing down the rocks to patrol the banks of the pool. With any luck, he would move on when he found the place deserted.

Moonlight broke through the clouds, and I pressed my back against the stones, sending frantic telepathic messages. *Don't turn around. Keep walking.* But he stopped. He bent to pick something up from the water's edge and turned it over in his hands. My vial. Great. That's just what I needed—a signal that someone's been here.

The assassin turned around. He lifted his head. I drew in a breath.

He was not a *he* at all.

I almost called out to her. After worrying about her being lost alone in the storm with a killer on the loose, the only thing my brain could accept was that she was here, safe. And then I focused on the gun in her hand.

In the ghostly light of the moon, Hisako's mouth curved into a wicked smile as she held up my pepper spray. "I know you are here, Elena," she called. "It is no use to hide."

I sank back against the stones, my mind reeling. Wait. Was Hisako working with Watts? Or was she the real hit man? Hit woman? Hit person? Had she killed Bianca? Was she trying to kill my dad? I couldn't believe it was true. All those questions she asked earlier . . . she'd been using me to get at the Mulos! I shook my head. It couldn't be real. And yet, there she was, and she wasn't going to go away.

Disbelief quickly turned to anger. I narrowed my eyes at her dark shape. No way was I going to let her get away with this.

Watching her from the shadows, I considered my limited options. If Hisako got close enough to realize it was me she'd been chasing, she might just head back down to the Plantation House and waste the real Elena Mulo. Then she'd kill Dr. Mulo, who wouldn't be able to save my dad. And what about Darlene? And Seth. No, I couldn't let that happen. I didn't have much time to think it through, but an idea formed in my head. It could work. . . .

Eventually, Hisako climbed back up the rocks and tossed the vial aside. She scanned the area again before heading back toward the trees. Just a little bit farther and I could make my move. I edged away from the stones, praying that my luck would hold. I tiptoed to the ledge. When I was in good diving position, I kicked at a loose stone.

It worked. The noise caught Hisako's attention, and she spun to face me. She raised her gun.

Then, out of nowhere, came a dark shape, flying straight at me. I screamed. A shot echoed through the cove as the shape slammed into me, hurtling us both over the edge.

Seth.

The force of the impact knocked the breath from me, and I didn't have time to take another before we plunged into the water. I sank downward in the blackness, pulled by the weight of Mrs. Mulo's coat. My lungs were already burning as I wriggled out of it and let it drift away. Even without the extra burden, I knew I was in trouble. If I popped back up to the surface to take a breath, I was dead. If I didn't get air, I was dead. My only chance was to get to the cave. Seth brushed by me, and I tugged on his arm, signaling for him to follow.

The waterfall churned above my head as I groped along the rocks, desperately feeling for the opening. I forced the small amount of air in my lungs into my mouth and then swallowed it again to give myself more time. It prolonged the inevitable a few more seconds, but that was not nearly enough. A small stream of bubbles escaped my lips as my chest constricted. Sparks of light danced in my vision. My ears began to ring. With a strange sense of calm, I realized that I wasn't going to make it.

It was then that Seth's hand closed around mine and he pulled me close. I tried to push away, but my strength, like the oxygen, was gone. Weakly, I tried to signal that we needed to find the entrance to the cave. He didn't seem to be getting the message. Instead, his free hand snaked around the back of my head. He drew me to him.

I've never felt such an electric shock pass through my body as when his lips touched mine. Every muscle, every nerve came alive, even as my life was slipping away.

I returned his kiss, parting my lips and letting my tongue slide tentatively along his. And then . . .

He pinched my nose and blew a breath into my mouth.

Too shocked at first to take it in, I pulled back, eyes opened wide. He grabbed me again and gave me another breath. I could feel my head clearing, which wasn't such a great thing, because now that I could think straight, I felt like a total idiot.

Seth was buddy-breathing, not kissing me. What a fool. What a . . .

I didn't have time to worry about it. Above our heads came a watery *plink!* followed by a zinging noise. Hisako was shooting into the water. I didn't know if she could see us in the darkness or if she was just shooting randomly into the pool, but either way, we were like the proverbial fish in a barrel.

I grabbed Seth's hand again and pulled him to where I hoped the opening was. Nothing. Solid rock. Another shot zinged by very close. I started to panic. Disoriented from the fall from the ledge and from the lack of oxygen, I had completely lost my bearings. It was too dark to see clearly among the shadows. Either we were going to drown, or Hisako was going to shoot us. Neither option sounded particularly appealing.

Seth pulled me close again. I shook my head. He couldn't keep breathing for me, giving up his own air. With an exasperated grunt, he grabbed my hand and slapped it against the rocks, then moved it downward so that I could feel the emptiness below. The tunnel! Without hesitation, I dove for it and wriggled my way through.

It wasn't until I had surfaced in the cave and sucked in a lungful of sweet, cool air that I began to worry about Seth. If it was tricky for 110-pound me to get through the opening, how was he, with his broad shoulders and football physique, ever going to make it?

I took a deep breath and dived back under, feeling along the rocks until I found Seth. He was straining to push himself through the opening, his muscles rigid and his chest all puffed up with the breath he was holding.

I pounded on his torso and blew out a mouthful of air. The bubbles burbled to the surface. Seth continued to struggle. He wasn't getting my message. I knocked on his chest again. *Exhale, stupid!*

As if he could hear my thoughts, he released his breath so that he had just enough give to push the rest of the way through. We came out of the water at the same time, our dual gasps for air echoing through the blackness of the cave.

I dragged myself out of the water, coughing and sputtering as I rolled onto my back on the cold, hard rocks. Seth flopped down beside me. I couldn't see him in the dark, nor was I touching him, but I could feel he was there. The energy radiated from him like an electromagnet, surrounding me, vibrating through me. Just like our underwater kiss. Or *unkiss*.

My face burned as I thought of what I had done. What was I thinking? *Sure, Seth. You're trying to save me? Here. Let me stick my tongue in your mouth.* Stupid, stupid, stupid! I could just imagine what must be going through his head. He would probably rag me about what I'd done. That thought made me want to hit him. Especially when it occurred to me that the whole thing was his fault anyway, so I shouldn't be the one feeling dumb.

I sat up and glared through the darkness to where I knew he was lying. "Well, I hope you're happy."

He grunted.

"I had everything under control. All I had to do was

let Hisako take a shot at me so I could fall into the water. I would have disappeared into the cave, and she'd have thought I was dead. But then you had to come along and try to be the big hero. You just about got us both killed!"

Again he grunted, which made me even angrier.

"One disappearing body she might have bought," I raged, "but two? She's going to figure out where we are. Caves behind waterfalls are not that uncommon. What happens when she comes after us? Did you think about that? Did you think at all?"

This time he didn't make a sound.

"See? You have no answer to that, do you?"

Silence.

"Seth?"

I reached for him in the dark. His arm lay right next to me. Limp. I followed it up to his shoulder. His neck. My fingers moved up over his face, reading his features like Braille. He was out cold.

And he was deathly still.

My heart dropped as I realized he wasn't breathing. Leaning close, I felt along his neck for a pulse and panicked when I couldn't find one. "No! Oh, no. Seth!"

I shook him hard. "Come on, come on." Kneeling beside him, I put my ear to his chest to listen for his heartbeat. What I felt about stopped my own heart cold.

Hot. Wet. Blood.

I bolted upright and fumbled with his shirt, ripping it away and feeling for where the blood was coming from.

The coppery smell of it filled the air. My fingers found an oozing hole on his left arm, just below his shoulder.

The shot. Right before we fell. Ice gripped my chest when I realized that Seth must have taken the bullet. He had saved my life. Again. No way was I going to sit there and let him die.

I grabbed his face. "Seth!"

Hands trembling, I tilted his head back, lowering his chin to make sure his airway was clear. With a strange sense of déjà vu, I pinched his nose and sealed my lips over his to give him a breath. It was a lot harder on a real person than on the dummies they use for lifeguard certification. I had to try several times before I could feel his chest rise. I gave him another quick breath and switched positions to start chest compressions.

I'm not ashamed to admit that I was all kinds of scared, not the least of which was the knowledge that there was an assassin lurking nearby ready to kill us. My immediate fear, though, was not knowing what to do with Seth. What if the CPR got his heart pumping stronger just so he could bleed to death from the gunshot wound? The rational part of me knew that wasn't likely, but I was way beyond rational by then.

I wished my dad were with me. I wished Seth's dad was with him. I wished I could talk to my mom. I wished for a whole lot of things as I counted compressions. The Red Cross says thirty, hard and fast, between rescue breaths.

That's hard work. I pumped rhythmically. Overwhelmed. Exhausted. Terrified.

"Please," I whispered into the darkness, "please don't let him die."

CHAPTER
13

Emotions that had been trapped inside for too long came tumbling out as I struggled to keep Seth alive. I vaguely remember tears, but I don't know exactly who they were for. Perhaps for Seth. More likely for myself.

Something about being responsible for another person's life thrusts your own under the microscope. You feel small, inadequate. At least I did. Every fault, every shortcoming magnified until I knew I wasn't worthy. I would screw up yet again, and Seth would die.

"Come on, Seth." Pump, pump, pump, pump. "Keep fighting." Strong breath. Listen. Strong breath. Pump, pump, pump, pump.

I kept giving him chest compressions and rescue breaths for I don't know how long. My head grew light, my muscles tight and weak, but I continued. I never realized it would be such exhausting work. And still no response from Seth.

"Seth! Please! Don't give up!"

I kept up an endless monologue. Mostly it was for my own benefit, but I hoped somewhere in his subconscious Seth could hear me. Maybe if he knew how I really felt about him, he might fight harder. I just hoped it wasn't too late to admit it.

Pump, pump, pump, pump. Twenty-seven, twenty-eight, twenty-nine, thirty. Big breath. Listen. Big breath.

"Too late" was the story of my life. I thought of my dad lying on the couch in his office, and new tears rolled down my cheeks. All these years I had been so fixated on the mom who had gone that I'd never let myself get close to the dad who had stayed. So, all right, maybe my dad did have a hand in her leaving, but we could work that out. At least I knew now that she hadn't gone because she didn't want me. That meant more to me than anything. If we ever got out of this mess, things were going to be different. All I needed was another chance.

Pump, pump, pump. Big breath. Big breath.

Seth had reached a part of me I'd kept hidden for years. He saw right through the walls I'd built to keep people out. I thought of his easy smile and gentle humor. Of how he'd made me feel, standing there in the storm. Letting my guard down hadn't been scary. It felt ... good. Right.

I bent to give him another breath, and for the first time, I was sure I felt a response, a movement of his lips. He had my full attention now. "Seth?" I listened for a heartbeat. Nothing. I breathed for him again, feeling his chest rise and fall. Laid my head on his chest to listen for the heartbeat once more. Thunk, thunk. Thunk, thunk.

It was faint, maybe a little erratic, but it was definitely there.

"Yes! That's it! Come on!"

I still couldn't tell if he was breathing on his own. I covered his mouth with mine and forced air into his lungs. Thunk, thunk. Thunk, thunk.

Again, I breathed for him.

And his lips did move. Unmistakably. Everything in the world narrowed to that point of contact between his lips and mine. Awakening. Life. Now I knew I was crying.

I sat up, wiping my eyes with the back of my hand, and tried to laugh. "I hope you don't think that qualified as our first kiss."

He coughed. I took that as a good sign.

"I'll need one when you're well. A kiss, I mean. To make up for all the trouble you've caused."

His hand closed over mine. "I'll . . . think . . . about it."

I wanted to dance, to sing, to swim, to laugh. But we weren't out of the woods yet. There was still the matter of Seth's gunshot wound. Not to mention Hisako, who was waiting outside to kill us both. Seth needed medical attention, and we were trapped. Somehow we had to get out of this cave.

"Seth, I'm going to go for help."

His hand tightened, squeezing on my fingers. "Don't . . . go."

"But you're hurt. If we don't—"

"I'll be . . . okay. Just . . . need rest."

I hesitated. Everything I knew about first aid told me I should seek immediate attention for Seth. But the first-aid rules don't generally take into consideration an assassin trying to hunt you down and kill you. If I left Seth, and something happened to me, who would know where to look for him? He could lay up there all alone and die. That didn't seem like the best scenario for either of us. I was going to have to take him with me, but until he was stronger, that wasn't going to happen either.

I propped my back against the cave wall and let Seth's head rest on my lap. And no, it wasn't quite as romantic as it sounds. I was keeping steady pressure on his wound, which, to be honest, was pretty gross. Plus, we were both cold and wet, and scared. Or at least I was. I can't tell you what Seth was thinking, because, as you may imagine, he was rather quiet.

I didn't feel like talking, anyway. I was too busy beating myself up. For someone who prides herself on reading people, I had missed Hisako by a long shot.

"Aphra?" Seth felt for my hand again.

"Yeah?"

"I'm sorry."

"What? No. Listen, I didn't mean what—"

"I mean . . . for coming here. We . . . should never have come . . . to your island."

"But I'm glad you did," I said softly.

His grip on my hand relaxed. "So what . . . do we do . . . now?"

"I don't know. Hisako could still be out there."

"What? Your friend?"

"Not anymore."

Seth tried to sit up. "I don't understand."

I pushed him back down. "Save your strength."

"I'm fine." He struggled upright again, but the way he groaned told me he was far from fine.

"You just about drowned! And in case you haven't noticed, you've been shot!"

"It's just . . . a flesh wound."

"What is this, Monty Python? Lie still."

"I thought you said . . . she was still out there. That she would . . . figure out where we were."

He was right. "Well, we'll just have to find another way out." I hoped there was another way. I'd only come in through the pool before. But then, I had never attempted to climb to the upper chamber because there were hordes of bats up there. Those bats had to get in and out somehow, though, right? That meant there had to be another opening. Problem was, I'd have to join the bats to find it. "You wait here. I'll climb up there and find a way out, then I'll come back to get you."

"I'm coming . . . with you."

"No. Are you crazy? You'll start bleeding again."

"I won't let you . . . go alone. It could be . . . dangerous."

"You're very gallant. But listen to yourself. You don't even have the energy to complete an entire sentence without pausing. You really think you're going to be able to protect me? Let's get real. I'm going to tie your shirt around your arm . . . there. It feels like it stopped bleeding, but you don't want to take any chances, so keep it elevated and—"

"I'm coming with you."

"What is it about this concept that you're not getting? You stay here, and I'll go look for—"

"I. Am. Coming. With. You."

"Seth, don't be an idiot. There's no way—"

From outside came a crash, followed by another.

"She knows we're in here," Seth said in a low voice.

"Don't worry," I whispered. "She can't get in."

"What's to stop her from going through the pool?"

"If she does that, we'll pounce her when she comes up on this side."

"It's pitch black in here. We'd never see her."

"Then she couldn't see us, either."

"Unless she has a flashli—"

Another crash. What was she doing? Trying to claw her way in? I didn't want to wait to find out.

"Okay, you win. Let's go."

CHAPTER
14

My plan was simple: to get Seth far enough away from the front of the cavern that Hisako couldn't see him if she somehow got inside. Then I'd figure out what to do next.

We felt our way up the clammy, sloping rock to the back of the cavern. Seth's breathing came in raspy fits, and he had to sit down every few feet. I was beginning to wonder if what we were doing was such a good idea. The back of the cave was blacker than a bat's behind. I had no idea where we were going or what lay ahead. Of course, the alternative was to do nothing, and that didn't seem like such a good idea, either.

As we climbed farther, the ceiling of the front chamber dropped so that I could feel the cold, damp rock just above my head. Before long, we had to crouch, and then crawl as the passage became shorter and shorter. Then the texture of stone beneath us abruptly changed. Coarse fragments in the rock bit into my hands and knees.

"Great." I muttered.

"What is it?"

"I'm not sure, but this feels like *pahoehoe*. It's a kind of lava rock. This is not going to be fun to cross."

"Wait." I heard tearing sounds and then Seth touched

my leg. "Give me your hands." I reached back, and he handed me some strips of his shirt. "Wrap this around them."

I quickly did as he suggested, and then I made him sit still so I could wrap his shoulder back up with the remains. The fabric helped some, but my hands still hurt. Of course, I wasn't about to complain. Seth was keeping pace with me over the same rough rock even though he had to gimp along like a three-legged dog.

The ceiling continued to drop. Before long we'd have to make like soldiers and crawl on our elbows. It would not be easy for him. He was already breathing heavily, so it was probably a good time for him to rest.

"Wait here," I said. "I'm going to go scout ahead and see where this leads."

This time he didn't argue, and that scared me. Either he was giving up, or he was too far gone to care. Fueled by the fear, I crawled forward again. I had to find a way out. For Seth.

The walls seemed to be closing in on me. Literally. Not because I was freaking out or anything. I really could feel the passage getting narrower and narrower until I realized that I must be in a sort of lava tube. How many tubes might run throughout the cave, I had no idea. I tried not to panic. I couldn't see a thing in there. What if I made a wrong turn going back to get Seth and got stuck in a maze of tubes forever?

I called out to him. "Seth?"

"Here! Did you . . . find anything?"

"Not yet. I'm still looking."

I breathed a little easier. At least if I could hear him, I could find my way back to that spot.

I pressed on. The rocks continued to narrow until I had just enough room to lay flat, cheek pressed against the rough, cold stone. And then my hand hit solid rock ahead. Dead end.

My eyes stung with tears of frustration. All that work for nothing. I was going to have to try another route, and we didn't have much time. But then I discovered an even bigger problem. As I tried to push myself back, I found that the space was too tight, and I couldn't move enough to turn around. Cold fear caught in my throat.

"Seth?" I called. "I need help."

Silence.

"Seth? Are you okay?"

More silence.

The fear intensified. My heart began to race uncomfortably. I was alone and blind and stuck under several tons of rock. Despite the chill, I began to sweat. My chest tightened up. I couldn't breathe. I could feel the beginnings of a full-on panic attack. But that wouldn't do Seth or me any good. I closed my eyes—not that it made a difference in the blackness of the cave—and made myself breathe deeply.

Think.

I had been crawling straight forward, no twists or

turns. It stood to reason that if I just backed up, I would find Seth. And once I did, I would have to get smarter about finding the nearest exit. If there were indeed several lava tubes in the cave, I'd better figure out a strategy for choosing the right one.

Again, I thought of the bats.

I have to tell you that just thinking about those things makes my skin crawl. I'm not talking about a surface fear. I am *terrified* of them. It's not rational. And it didn't make my realization any easier.

Bats are nocturnal hunters, which meant that, at that very moment, they would be winging their way in and out of the cave through some opening somewhere. To get out of the cave, I would have to follow the bats. But since I couldn't see where that opening might be, I would have to adapt their sonar sense to find the way out. I had to become one with them. I might have laughed at the irony if I hadn't been so disgusted.

If I could just get back to Seth, we could listen for the bats together. Problem was, I was stuck, and I had no idea where Seth was. Or where I was, for that matter. But now I had hope, and that gave me enough courage to try again. By lifting up on my toes, I was able to gain enough leverage to inch backward. My shirt got shredded, and the rock raked my stomach, but at least I was moving. Finally, the ceiling raised enough that I could sit. I turned around and crab-walked to where I thought Seth would be.

He wasn't there.

"Seth? Where are you?"

Nothing. And I couldn't see him. I couldn't even see my own hands if I held them right in front of my face. The panic started to set in again.

I reached out. "Seth?" I moved a little to my left. Nothing. A little more. Nothing. I struck out blindly. "Come on. This isn't funny."

Finally I felt my foot touch something soft. I nudged it. "Seth?"

"Unh . . ."

It's hard to describe the relief I felt at that moment. I almost started to cry again.

"Did you . . . ," he said groggily. "The opening . . ."

"Not yet," I said. "But I think I know how to find it now."

We sat very still and listened. Behind us, the falls rushed over the cliff and into the pool. Nearer, water dripped steadily on stone. And ahead to the left came the agitated rustling of tiny bodies. My insides curdled while, at the same time, I felt giddy with relief.

"Come on. This way."

Seth and I slowly, carefully, crawled toward the sound. The way was narrow, but the sounds grew louder as we pressed forward. Finally, the darkness faded into lesser shades of black. Somewhere ahead, light was getting into the cave. There must be an opening!

Unfortunately, the bats began to sense our presence, and they weren't happy. They started making anxious squeaking noises and shifting around. I gritted my teeth and tried to shut out the sound. Something brushed against my hair. Instinctively, I raised my hand to swat it away. Big mistake. I aroused protective bat mamas who swooped at me, leathery wings beating the air, furry little bodies bumping against me, tiny feet catching my hair.

I threw my arms over my head. This only caused the bats to become even more agitated.

"Be still!" Seth's voice hissed from the darkness.

"I am!"

He grabbed my hand and pulled me to him. I tried to focus only on my contact with Seth and to ignore the creatures flying around my head. For the first time, I was glad for the darkness so that he couldn't see that I was crying again.

It seemed to take forever, but eventually the bats settled down. Now all I had to do was crawl through their domain. No problem. Tentatively, I placed a hand down on the rock in front of me . . . right onto something squishy and cold. Bat poop. I recoiled, wiping my hand on my pants. "Ugh! That's nasty!"

"Don't be a wimp."

Wimp? I don't think so. I crawled right through the middle of the bat colony. Over the gushy, guano-covered rocks. The smell was overwhelming. More than once I thought I was going to lose it, but I wasn't about to give Seth the satisfaction.

Finally—and just in time—I caught a whiff of fresh air. Outside air. It was enough to keep me going. The blackness turned to gray. I could see dark shapes darting through the air ahead. Through the ceiling.

I don't believe I have ever been as happy to see the night sky as I was when I reached that opening. Eagerly, I stood and wriggled through. Ghosts of clouds were all that remained of the storm. Stars sparkled as if the gods had tossed a handful of glitter into the air. Moonlight frosted the rocks around me in a silvery wash. It was the most beautiful thing I had ever seen.

From my narrow ledge of rock, I could look out over the tops of the jungle trees and down toward the valley. Toward home. I closed my eyes and thanked the bats.

The next problem would be figuring out where we were going to go from there. On one side of the cliff, I could hear the steady rush of the waterfall. On the other side, the rocks looked loose and unstable. Above me, slabs of stone jutted outward in a way that would make climbing up impossible.

It would have to be down, then.

Down to where Hisako was waiting with her gun.

CHAPTER 15

Seth was in no condition to go rock climbing. His arm was weak from the gunshot, and he was still a little woozy from the drowning thing. But there was no alternative.

With the trees below and the way the rock face was situated, we couldn't see all the way down to the clearing. I hoped that meant Hisako could not see us. With luck, the sound of the waterfall would also drown out any noise that we made.

"You keep a lookout while I climb," I told Seth, "and I'll watch while you climb."

He just nodded and peered over the ledge. A little cautiously, I thought.

"Don't tell me you're afraid of heights."

"Hah!" He gave me an arrogant tough-guy look, but I noticed that he didn't deny the acrophobia.

"Don't worry." I felt among the vines that clung to the cliff face to find some sturdy enough to support our weight. "I climb up here all the time." Of course, when I go rock climbing, I use the proper gear, but I wasn't going to tell him that. "Besides, we're just climbing from one ledge to another. It's not really that far if you look at it that way."

He gave me a dark look.

"I'm just saying."

The drop to the next ledge was probably only about eight feet, but I worried that, with Seth's shoulder, he wouldn't be able to climb even that far. I climbed down first. Not that I'd be able to catch him if he fell or anything like that, but at least I could try to guide him to the next foothold.

As it was, I shouldn't have worried. Seth had the natural grace of an athlete, and even though his left arm dangled uselessly at his side, he made it to the next level without a problem—except for the amount of strength it took from him. He looked like he was going to pass out. I pulled him away from the ledge. "How 'bout we sit for a minute."

He shook his head. "I'm fine."

"Stop already. What is it that you're trying to prove? That you can be tough? Okay, I believe you. Now sit."

He sat, but only because he was getting too weak to stand. I knelt beside him and checked his shoulder. Now that I could see it in the moonlight, I was even more amazed that he'd made it this far. The bullet had passed straight through his arm. The skin around the puckered wounds was puffy and swollen, like a rising omelet. I was careful not to let the shock show on my face as I tied the torn shirt around it neatly.

"You're going to want to have your dad look at that."

He nodded.

I sat next to him and looked out over the moonlit trees. "I've never been up here at night. It's kinda peaceful."

He wasn't as impressed. "We need to get down."

I figured he was just nervous on account of the height thing, and I tried to reassure him.

He scowled. "I was thinking of my parents. They're still not safe."

"Oh." I looked down at my hands. The silence stretched between us. Finally I got up the nerve to ask. "Who are you running from, Seth?"

"A crazy woman with a gun."

"Funny. Who sent her? Why is she after you?"

"Huh. And here I thought you knew it all."

"My guess is you're hiding from the Mob."

He bunched up his shoulders and looked away.

"Tell me. Who's your family hiding from? Does it have something to do with organized crime?"

His voice took on a tone I hadn't heard before. "It's bigger than that."

"Bigger than a crime cartel? Because that's pretty big."

"As big as an entire government?"

"What?"

He snorted. "You had no clue, did you? 'Oh, I know all about you and your family, Seth,'" he mimicked.

"Hey. I said I knew you weren't who you were claiming to be. I never said I knew why."

He shot me a sharp look. "Because we don't know who to trust anymore."

I touched his arm. "You can trust me."

"That's what they said."

"Look around, Seth. Who am I going to tell your secrets to?"

He regarded me for a moment, and then dropped his gaze. When he looked up again, I could tell he had made up his mind to confide in me, but I wasn't sure if the decision was born of assurance or defeat. "I don't know all the details." He drew in a deep breath, like this story was going to take some effort to tell. "I didn't know anything, as a matter of fact, until I was thirteen. My name was Dylan then."

He didn't look like a Dylan to me, but I didn't want to say anything to stop the flow. I just nodded.

"They pulled me out of school one afternoon. Said we were going on an early vacation and headed straight for the airport. We ended up in Michigan. That's where I found out my whole life was a lie." He ran a hand through his hair, looking at once bewildered and lost. It was all I could do to keep from reaching up and smoothing the hair back down again.

"My real name wasn't Dylan," he said softly. "That was the name they gave me when they moved us the first time. I don't remember that. They said I used to be Mikhael."

"That's a nice name." Stupid, but I didn't know what else to say.

His face clouded. "They recruited my parents, you know. And now it's like they want to get them killed."

"Who?"

"The government."

I realized my mouth was hanging wide open and closed it. "Wait. Our government? Why?"

He shook his head and looked away. He didn't say anything for a long time. I laid a tentative hand on his arm. He looked into my eyes then, as if trying to see if I was really worthy of his trust.

Finally, he spoke. "You know what sleeper cells are, right?"

"Of course."

"My mom and dad used to be part of one."

My mouth dropped open again. "No way."

"Yeah. They don't talk much about it, but from what I understand, when they first came over, they weren't even married. It was just a cover. To be together, you know? And then . . ."

"They fell in love," I breathed. You have to admit that was romantic.

"And then I came along." He picked up a rock and ran his thumb along the rough edges. "They knew they had to do something." He glanced up at me. "Having a kid changed everything for them. They wanted out, but they knew they would never be allowed to just walk away from the program. And then they found out they wouldn't be able to keep me, either. That's when they defected."

I sucked in a breath. "And they went to the government."

He nodded. "They agreed to give the U.S. government information in exchange for protection. That's when they entered the Witness Protection Program the first time . . . but not before my mom fingered one of the cell leaders. He was a big catch for the government because his minions had infiltrated about every level of intelligence there was. They called him 'The Mole.'

"It wasn't long before the CIA came knocking. Mom and Dad knew a lot of people and a lot of secrets, and the government wanted in. The whole time we were living in California, I thought my dad was in exotic-car sales. He was really working for the CIA."

"Then what happened?"

"The Mole escaped."

"Oh."

"Yeah. That's when my mom and dad knew the CIA could no longer protect them. So they left. We moved to Michigan, and I became Seth."

"And now?"

He gave me a look like I was as dumb as the rock he held in his hand. "The Mole found us."

I had to take a minute to let it all sink in. "But what does that have to do with Hisako?"

Seth shrugged. "I'm sure this guy doesn't do his own dirty work."

"So she's his hit man."

"That would be my guess."

"Can't you go back to the CIA and ask for protection again?"

"My dad thinks it was someone in the agency who gave us up."

I could only shake my head. "But . . . why?"

Seth shrugged. "All I know is what my dad said. That if they didn't think we were already dead, they'd kill us themselves."

I sat still for a moment, digesting what he had told me and wondering how my mom figured into the equation. "Is my mom with the CIA?"

He didn't answer me.

"Is that how you came to us? Did she send you?"

His hand closed over mine. "You can never say I told you. Promise?"

I didn't dare breathe. "I promise."

"She was our contact in the CIA. I never knew that until I was older; I just thought she was a family friend. And she *was* a friend. She kept in touch even after she had been reassigned, which I guess is strictly forbidden. She was the one who came and got us when The Mole escaped." He looked into my eyes. "Four years ago."

I swear, my heart stopped beating. Four years. That was when we came to the island.

"That's all I know."

I murmured my thanks. There were still a lot of questions, but his story explained a lot. My mom hadn't left to find herself; she had gone to save a family. I only hoped it wasn't too late to save ours.

I stared down at his large hand folded over my smaller one and blinked away the tears. "One last question. With all those identities . . . which name do you prefer?"

He thought for a moment. "Seth, I guess. It's been too long since I've answered to anything else."

"Okay . . . Seth."

He squeezed my fingers, and the edge of his garnet ring bit into my skin. "You know, I have to tell you"—I tried to make my voice bright to lighten the mood—"this ring of yours has got to be the ugliest thing I have ever seen."

"I'm insulted." He held his hand up to the moonlight and straightened the monstrosity on his finger. "My dad gave this to me when we moved to Michigan. 'To remember the old life,' he said. I've never taken it off. I look at it and see California."

"Remind me never to visit California."

He slugged me. Softly, though. "We should go."

Seth still had to take a break between every ledge, but bit by bit we worked our way down the rocks. It was never easy, and once we got below the tree line it got even scarier. We could see the clearing then, well lit in the moonlight. I only hoped that if Hisako was down there she wouldn't look up, because if she did, she'd be sure to see us.

Every time I went over the side, I felt like I had a huge bull's-eye painted on my back. I was an open target for Hisako, wherever she was.

Finally, we made it to the ground. It wasn't pretty, but we did it.

After we rested again, Seth took my hand once more, and we crept through the shadows. I tried not to read too much into the hand-holding, but it made me happy just the same. Moonlight shone in patches through the trees, shifting as the branches moved with the lingering wind. Dodging those patches, we wove our way through the soggy undergrowth toward the clearing.

Something dull and white lay on the ground ahead. I squinted through the shadows. My vial of pepper spray! It seemed like a lifetime ago I had lost it. Could it have only been earlier that afternoon? The vial rested on its side. When we got closer, I could see that the top had broken off and most of the contents had spilled out. It lay nestled among the leaves of a Star of Bethlehem plant. Hisako's favorite, I thought grimly. Then I stopped.

"Wait a minute." I stooped down and grabbed the vial.

"What are you doing?" Seth asked.

"Hold on."

I crawled down to the water's edge and filled the broken vial with water, careful not to lose the small remains of the pepper spray. When I returned to the plant, I broke off a stem and stuck the torn end into the vial. I made sure not to get any of the milky sap on my skin.

"I don't get it," Seth whispered.

"You will. I'm trying to—"

"Do not move." Hisako's voice sent creepie-crawlies down my spine.

CHAPTER
16

Seth moved protectively in front of me. It made me feel warm inside—or it would have, if I hadn't been staring down the barrel of a particularly nasty-looking pistol.

I tucked the vial behind the plant and raised my hands in surrender. "*Konbanwa*, Hisako."

Confusion passed over her face for a moment. She squinted through the shadows. "Aphra-*chan?*"

I nodded.

"So. It appears you have tricked me." She shifted the gun in her hand. "You were never the target, Aphra-*chan.*" She had the grace to look sorry as she added, "You have now made yourself such."

Seth tensed, his muscles taut like a coil ready to spring. I touched his arm, hoping he would get my message. *Not yet.* If I was going to catch her off guard, I had to stall, to wait for the moment. I only hoped she'd keep talking.

"What about my dad? What did he ever do to you?"

"That could not be helped." She turned to Seth. "If your father had tried to help the girl, Jack-*sama*'s demise would not have been necessary."

"What are you talking about?"

Hisako shook her head, as if she were surprised by our stupidity. "I was quite certain I could draw your father out of hiding if he could see that his doctoring skills were needed. But I underestimated him. He allowed the girl to die."

Seth tensed. "No. You're wrong."

Hisako shot him a contemptuous look and continued. "Surely if his host became ill, I thought, he would risk exposure to help him . . ."

"But how?" Understanding dawned before I finished the question. "The plants. You drugged him."

The triumphant look on her face told me I was right.

"You're sick!"

She blinked. "Did you not employ the same methods to dispose of Watts-*sama?*"

Now Seth shot me a look, and he shifted slightly. Away from me.

"No! The plants I used were to put him to sleep. Not permanently. Just . . . until . . ."

"Aphra-*chan*. Didn't you wonder at his illness when he arrived? I had already arranged for him to receive a small . . . token of my esteem, shall we say, before he boarded the helicopter to come to the island. Combined with your creation . . ."

I felt the blood drain from my face. She'd used me. Again. But I wasn't going to sit there and take it like the meek little eager-to-please Aphra I had once been. Not after the weekend I'd had.

I felt behind me with one hand until my fingers wrapped around the vial. "Hisako?" She turned her attention to me. I sprang to my feet and threw the plant-sap-firewater in her face.

She screeched and clawed at her eyes, inadvertently dropping the gun.

"Grab it! Grab it!" I ran at Hisako, knocking her to the ground. Straddling her chest, I smacked her hard on one side of the face and then the other, all my anger welling up inside and coming out through my fists.

Seth pulled me off her. "What are you doing? Come on! Let's go!"

I glanced back over my shoulder as he dragged me into the woods. Hisako howled like a she-wolf and groped about, unable to open her eyes. There was still fight left in her. Plenty of fight. Maybe we should have finished her off. The thought made me sick to my stomach.

We hadn't gone far before Seth had to slow to a walk to catch his breath.

"You . . . have security . . . at the resort?"

"Just a night watchman. Our head of security got stuck in the city last night."

"Is the watchman armed?"

I looked at the gun in Seth's hand. "He is now."

"She might have more weapons." His voice was grim.

I hoped he was wrong.

• • •

It didn't take long to reach the edge of the taro patch. Seth jumped down into the muck first and reached back to help me down. This time, I accepted his chivalry.

"Wow, such a gentleman."

He raised a brow. "You say that as if you're surprised."

"Only a little."

I couldn't help but notice that he hadn't let go of my hand. I smiled up at him. He smiled back.

The sound of a gunshot tore through our peaceful cocoon. Hisako stood on the bank, a miniature revolver leveled at me. So Seth was right about the other weapon.

He raised his gun, but she fired at him, knocking it from his hand. It hit the water with a splash. She turned her glare on me, eyes swollen, tears flowing freely down her cheeks. My heart dropped. The plant juice had not blinded her after all.

Seth and I exchanged a quick look. Hisako would not waste her breath monologuing this time; we were in trouble. I glanced pointedly at the water, and he inclined his head. Hisako directed her aim at me. I took a deep breath and dropped beneath the surface before she had time to fire. The bullet *ploinked* into the sludge above me. One one-thousand, two-one-thousand . . . I slid under the muck toward her, praying that she would play her part. I could feel Seth somewhere nearby. The knowledge soothed my nerves and gave me the strength for what I had to do next.

The human brain is a funny thing. It's conditioned to base expectancy on experience. Above me on the shore, I imagined that Hisako would be scanning the taro field, waiting for us to surface. Reason would tell her we couldn't stay under much longer. Of course, up at the cove she had seen us disappear into the pool, but she probably figured we had found someplace to hide. This time there were no hiding places except the leaves of the taro plants. The direction we would reasonably go would be far away from her. With luck, when she didn't see us come up for air, she would take the bait and hunt us down.

As I had hoped, I felt the water slosh as she jumped into the bog. She would be ahead of me now. I zeroed in on her location, then sprang up from the water to tackle her from behind.

She must have sensed me coming. At the last moment, she spun, foot sloshing through the rancid water as she kicked up and hit me square in the chest. I stumbled backward and landed on the row of taro plants, gripping the stems to keep from falling under. I wheezed for breath and tried to stand. She steadied her stance to take aim at me once more. At that moment, Seth jumped at her from the other side. He wrestled away the pistol, but not without a fight. She slugged him on the chin and followed through with an elbow. Seth fell into the water. She lunged at him.

I reacted by instinct. Yanking on the stem in my

hands, I pulled out a taro root and swung the football-size corm at Hisako's head. It knocked her sideways long enough for Seth to regain his balance. He used the momentum to push her off her feet. She landed facedown in the water. He grabbed the back of her head in his one good hand, holding it under.

Heart jumping crazily, I sloshed to where he was and helped to keep her down. She thrashed and bucked, much stronger than I had expected. A sick feeling curled around me. Could we really do this?

Eventually her struggles weakened. She went limp. I backed away, but Seth continued to hold her under.

"That's enough, Seth."

He didn't move.

"Seth!"

He blinked and let go. Hisako floated facedown in the water.

We dragged her body through the taro patch. My insides knotted tighter with every step. I'd never hurt anyone before.

"Hurry," I urged. "Help me get her on land."

We rolled Hisako's body out of the taro bog and climbed out after it. Seth bent over her.

"Is she breathing?" I asked.

He ran a worried hand over his face. "I don't think so."

"Help me lift her up." Trembling, I knelt behind her and grasped her around the ribs, driving my hand and fist upward into her abdomen in a Heimlich maneuver to make sure she didn't have any water or gunk in her lungs before I began CPR.

After about four good tries, Hisako coughed and sputtered. We laid her back down, listening to make sure she was breathing on her own. I lifted one eyelid. Her eyes were rolled back so that only the whites were showing.

"One of us should stand guard while the other goes for help," I said. "I'm the certified lifeguard, so I can stay with her."

"If you think I'm leaving you alone with a killer, you're crazy."

"She can't do anything while she's unconscious. Go. Hurry back before she wakes up."

He shook his head. "No way."

"Well, then, just what do you propose we do?"

Without a word, Seth grabbed her by the arms and pulled her into a sitting position. Bending down, he hoisted her onto his one good shoulder. Of course, then he didn't have enough strength to stand.

"What are you doing?" I pulled her limp body away from him. "You're *not* thinking of taking her with us."

"Why not?"

"This entire night was about keeping her away from the Plantation House. Why would we want to take her there now?"

"Well, we can't leave her here. And like you said, she can't do anything while she's unconscious. We'll just have to make sure she stays that way."

He was right, but I still didn't like it. I grumbled as much under my breath as we lashed together a kind of stretcher out of palm fronds and sticks and Madeira vines. We rolled Hisako onto the stretcher, and I wrapped a few extra vines around her hands and feet, just to be safe. Seth raised a brow at that and looked as if he were holding back a smile.

I huffed. "She wakes up, I'm letting her get you first."

Hisako may have been small, but she felt heavier with every step. The sticks we had used for the frame of her stretcher bit into my hands, and my fingers grew numb from gripping them. The muscles in my arms and across my shoulders strained and ached. Not that I was going to complain—Seth was carrying the same load with an injured shoulder. And I'm sure he longed for the same thing I did—for us to get down the hill and then to get as far away from Hisako as the island would allow.

Unfortunately, I had forgotten about the ravine.

Seth had been leading the way, and so I hadn't even been thinking about the route; I just followed behind. When his step slowed, I peered around him and immediately recognized the void ahead.

My stomach sank. "Great," I mumbled.

Seth glanced back over his shoulder. "What?"

"The ravine. I pushed the log off the ledge."

"No problem. We'll just—"

"It wouldn't have been easy hauling her across anyway, but without the log—"

"We don't need the log."

"What are we supposed to do? Swing across on vines? We're going to have to find another way. We—"

"Aphra," Seth cut in, "shut up, would you? Just follow me."

Like I had a choice. He led the way uphill along the lip of the ravine. The space between the two sides seemed to be getting narrower. Not seemed to, was. Huh. For all my exploring, I had never come up this far.

"How did you know?" I asked.

"How did you think I crossed it the first time?"

The gap narrowed until the two sides were two or three feet apart—close enough to jump, but far enough apart that you could still fall down into the crevice if you weren't careful. I swallowed dryly, remembering how the log had smashed when it hit the bottom.

"How are we going to do this?" I asked. "With Hisako, I mean."

"Very carefully," he said.

He set Hisako's stretcher down and I did the same. I flexed my fingers, trying to work some feeling back into them.

"Here's what we're going to do . . . " Seth sounded like he was making it up as he went along, but seeing as how I didn't have any better ideas, I was more than happy to give him the responsibility.

He cleared the gap in one easy jump, and then knelt

on the edge, facing me. He reached out a hand. "Okay. Slowly, now."

I pushed Hisako, feet first, toward him. Inch by inch, her stretcher extended over the void. The further out she got, the more the balance shifted until I had to practically sit on the handles to keep her from upending and toppling downward.

Finally, Seth was able to grab hold of her from the other side and pulled her toward him—quickly, not slow and careful like I had been doing. My breath caught as the end of the stretcher slipped out of my hands and off my side of the ravine, but just as quick, Seth had yanked her over to his side and sat panting as she lay, oblivious, beside him.

I took a couple of running steps and jumped over the gap to join them. In the fading moonlight, Seth's face looked especially pale. The fabric I had wrapped around his shoulder glistened darkly. He was bleeding again.

"Do you want to rest for a minute?" I asked.

His lips set into a grim line. "No. Let's just go." He pushed to his feet and picked up his end of the stretcher. I scrambled to do the same on my end, my hands past feeling by that point. Once again, I followed Seth through the jungle.

By the time we made it down the hill, the gray light of predawn lined the horizon. Soon a new day would be here, and this nightmare would be over.

Or so I thought.

Dr. Mulo was the first to see us coming. He had been standing near the lanai doors and nearly tore them off their hinges to get to us.

He helped Seth carry Hisako inside, checking her vitals along the way.

"This is your friend?" he asked me. "Your Hisako? What has happened to her?" They laid her on the wicker couch in the reception area. "Elena! The lamp!"

Mrs. Mulo quickly appeared at our sides, holding the lantern high. That's when she saw her son's arm. "Seth! What have you done?"

"It's nothing," he said. "I'm fine."

"That doesn't look like nothing to me."

"Really, I'm okay."

"Victor . . ."

"Elena, leave the boy alone." Dr. Mulo completed his examination of Hisako before turning to Seth himself. "Now," he said, "suppose you tell us what happened."

Seth gave him the SparkNotes version of the night's events, leaving out the part about his nearly dying, I noticed. When Seth told him who Hisako really was, his dad uttered what I am reasonably sure was a very bad swear word in his native tongue.

"My dad," I said. "Is he—?"

Mrs. Mulo laid a hand on my arm. "He'll be fine. He's resting."

I nodded, numb with relief. "I . . . I'm sorry I lost your coat."

"Coat? Aphra, I don't care about the coat. You could have been killed!" She shook her head. "Why? After all the worry we've caused, why would you do that for us?"

I straightened. My mom had shown me by example what it was to be strong. All those things we did together . . . she was teaching me, guiding me to be like her. Though I hadn't known it until a few hours ago, she had sacrificed everything to save the lives of the people she was sworn to protect. I realized that I had just done the same. Why would I do that? I raised my chin proudly.

Because I'm my mother's daughter.

CHAPTER
17

nce Hisako was taken care of, Dr. Mulo began to examine Seth's wound, and soon Mrs. Mulo's attention was drawn to what they were saying. I took the opportunity to slip away from them and go looking for my dad.

He wasn't in the office, though I found Darlene in there, slumped over the desk, snoring softly with her head on her arms. I tiptoed over and touched her shoulder.

Darlene startled and jumped up from the chair as soon as she saw it was me. "Oh, Aphra! Honey!" She nearly tackled me as she gathered me in her arms. Her shoulders shook as she hiccupped and sobbed. "I thought you were gone to us." She pulled back, cupping her hands around my cheeks. "Don't you ever sneak off like that again! I couldn't bear it if we lost you."

I wiggled free, assuring her I was fine. "Where's my dad? I need to talk to him."

She dabbed a tissue at her eyes. "Not until we get you cleaned up. He's had a rough night of it. Your Dr. Mulo says we shouldn't upset him. He'll have a heart attack as it is when he sees what you've done with your hair." She gingerly lifted an uneven lank and eyed it with disapproval.

Darlene said Dad was asleep in his bed. I did as she

said and took a quick shower. I toweled off, staring at my reflection in the mirror. It wasn't pretty. My face was covered with scratches and mosquito welts, and the dark shadows under my eyes made me look like some kind of ghoul. At least, if I slicked my hair back, he might not be able to tell how badly it had been hacked.

The first weak rays of morning sun lit my room as I dressed in clean clothes. Finally, as presentable as I was going to get, I tiptoed to my dad's door and cracked it open.

He lay on his bed, propped up with pillows. White gauze encircled his neck like a priest's collar. A plastic tube ran from the front of the bandages to some kind of contraption on his nightstand made out of mason jars and yet more tubing.

I stepped inside the room. The hinges squeaked, and I made a mental note that I really would have to get them fixed.

Slowly, Dad opened his eyes.

"Daddy!"

I couldn't help it. I ran to his bedside and laid my head on his chest, blubbering incoherently as he stroked my short, wet hair.

Only when Dad made a weird noise in his throat did I raise my head. "Are you all ri—" I followed his gaze to see Dr. Mulo and Seth standing at the door. Gripped with a sudden shyness, I lost my tongue. Dad motioned for them to come in.

Seth had cleaned up and changed into faded blue jeans and a soft white T-shirt. I would like to have gone to him to find out just how soft, but Darlene and Mrs. Mulo followed close behind.

"I told your father the truth about why we came here," Dr. Mulo said to me. "I think all the misunderstandings between us have been cleared up."

Dad nodded, though he grimaced in pain as he did so.

"Please, tell us once again what happened last night—for your father's benefit."

One more time, Seth and I recited the events as they had transpired, from the moment the lights went out at the Plantation House until we returned with Hisako, each filling in gaps that the other left out. I learned that Seth had seen me slip out into the storm and had followed me right from the start.

My dad listened silently—not that he could have talked if he'd wanted to—gesturing when he needed us to back up or explain something more clearly.

When we concluded, Dr. Mulo shook his head. "One thing I do not understand," he said. "Aphra, last night you warned us that we were in danger because a man had come to the island and was asking questions about us, and yet the alleged assassin lying on the couch downstairs is most assuredly a woman."

"Oh, no! I forgot all about Mr. Watts!"

At the mention of his name, Dad became very

agitated. He tried to speak more than once, but only managed choking noises. I rummaged through his desk drawer and grabbed him a note pad and a pencil.

Watts agency, he wrote.

"Oh. Oh, my." Darlene pressed her hands to her face. "Jack, is this the man you told me about?"

Dad nodded as best he could.

Looking from one to the other, Dr. Mulo asked, "What?"

Darlene cleared her throat. "Jack, uh . . . Wow, how do I say this? He called the CIA when you arrived."

Dr. and Mrs. Mulo exchanged grave looks.

"He was worried." Darlene rushed to explain. "You have to understand. Knowing the . . . *element* Natalie works with, he had to be sure you weren't dangerous. He called the agency to verify that Natalie had sent you."

Dr. Mulo shook his head. "She no longer works with the CIA."

Darlene worried the hem of her uniform blouse. "But . . . Watts was her partner."

Mrs. Mulo grasped her husband's arm. "Oh, Victor. If the agency found us, then—"

Mr. Mulo nodded. "The Mole won't be far behind." He turned to me. "Where is this man now?"

I shook my head. "I don't know. He wasn't where I left him. He couldn't have gone far, though. I . . . I kind of drugged him."

"You what?"

"Well . . ." I twisted my hands. "I thought he was after you. I just gave him something to help him sleep until you had a chance to get away." An awful feeling gnawed at my gut. "There's something else. I told Hisako about him, and she said she had already drugged him. What if what I gave him accidentally . . . um . . . finished him off?"

Dr. Mulo pressed his lips together. He turned to Mrs. Mulo with a grim look on his face. "Elena, come with me. Seth, you keep watch over Miss Shimizu."

"I'll have to show you where his villa is." I rose to my feet. Dad squeezed my hand, and I looked down at him, a lump rising in my throat. "I'll be right back."

We hurried down the path, the silence weighing on me every step of the way. I was afraid we'd walk into the villa and find Watts dead.

Dr. Mulo finally spoke as we turned off the main path. "What exactly did you use to drug this man?"

I told him as much as I could remember, and he nodded but said nothing.

We knocked on the door when we reached the villa, but, as expected, there was no answer. My hands trembled as I slid the master key into the lock. I opened the door but couldn't bring myself to go inside. Mrs. Mulo stood with me on the lanai as Dr. Mulo searched the premises.

He returned rather quickly, one hand to his face. Took me a moment to realize he was chuckling.

Seems I'd chosen a bad combination of herbs. Agent Watts had spent a very long night—not asleep, as I had intended, but in the loo with an awfully bad case of Kapua's revenge.

It must have chapped Watts to have his quarry right there in front of him and not be able to do anything about it. If he'd had the energy, I'm sure he would have attempted to drag the Mulos in right then like a good little agent.

As it was, his temporary weakness bought us some time. Not much, though. Frank had said Junior would be coming back from the city with the police. Now that the storm had passed, they could arrive at any moment. We hurried back to the Plantation House.

Mrs. Mulo leaned close to her husband. "We are no longer safe here."

I didn't like the sound of that. It felt like a nail being driven into a coffin. "You could hide. We can tell Agent Watts that you've already gone, and then once he leaves—"

She shook her head. "Both Hisako and Watts found us. Others could, too. It is time for us to move on."

As much as I didn't want to hear that, I knew she was right.

Dr. Mulo agreed. "We don't have much time. As soon as Agent Watts regains his strength, we are lost. We need to leave immediately, but how?"

"Frank can take you," I offered.

"No good. He has suffered a concussion. He's not fit to fly."

"Better not let him hear you say that. Frank's a combat veteran. I'm sure he's flown with worse than a bump on the head."

"Excellent." Dr. Mulo brightened. "Then I should check in on him now."

My shoulders drooped. I was going to have to stop volunteering information that would help send Seth away.

Back in the lobby, he stood guard over Hisako's prone body. I trudged over to join him. She was still sleeping, her eyes bandaged and the vines around her hands and feet replaced with nylon cording.

"My dad gave her a sedative," Seth said. "She should be out until the CIA comes to get her."

"If he's not openly practicing, where does your dad get this medication?"

Seth grimaced. "Don't ask."

I watched Hisako's sleeping face. She looked so innocent and peaceful when she was unconscious. "Do you think we did the right thing? What if she has some kind of permanent damage from oxygen deprivation or something?"

"I don't know what else we could have done. She was trying to kill us, Aphra. At least we didn't sink to her level. The authorities will take care of her."

"But how will they know to be prepared? To take her into custody, I mean. We've no phones, no power—"

"Hell, I already roused the cavalry." Frank stood on the stairs with Darlene close behind, fussing over him and holding an ice pack to his head.

"Hey, Frank. You feeling okay?"

"This thing? It's just a bump." He pushed aside the ice pack as if to illustrate his burliness. "I radioed Junior this morning. He's on his way with a whole passel of law folk."

Radio. I'd forgotten Frank had a short wave in his helicopter.

He looked to Seth. "Get your gear together. We'd better get moving."

"You're going to fly them to the city?" I asked.

"I'm goin' to fly 'em somewhere."

"So soon?"

"Way I hear it, there's no time to lose."

I felt hollow. It was all happening too fast. "I'll come help."

"Shouldn't you watch the lady?"

My heart sank. I wasn't ready to say good-bye to Seth just yet.

Darlene cleared her throat. "I'll watch. Go."

As it turned out, Frank didn't get much help from either Seth or me. We tried, but kept tripping over lines, fumbling with latches, and generally messing things up until he told us to get out of his way. We stood together on the landing pad, silent. There were just too many things to say and not enough time to say them.

Seth's parents arrived within just a few minutes, carrying their luggage. Mrs. Mulo wore a light blue floral-print dress and had brushed her hair into short, soft waves. Dr. Mulo had also gone casual, in jeans and a golf shirt. I liked them much better this way. They looked . . . regular.

Mrs. Mulo gave me a quick hug. "I want to tell you something," she whispered close to my ear. "I knew your mother well enough to know that she loves you very much. She'd be proud of what you've done." She tucked a piece of paper into my pocket. "I think you've earned this. I don't have to tell you how important it is that you keep it secret." She gave me another little squeeze, and with that she pulled away and climbed on board the helicopter, where Dr. Mulo already sat, motioning for Seth to join them.

The whine of the engines raised in pitch as the rotors began to move faster.

"All right," Frank yelled. "Let's go!"

My throat closed up. I could hardly breathe, let alone say good-bye. Biting my lip, I looked into Seth's eyes one last time.

"I have to go," he said.

I nodded, still unable to speak.

"Seth!" Dr. Mulo called.

"I guess this is good-bye," I managed to whisper.

"For now, anyway. Remember, I know where you live."

I laughed. "I'll never forget you, Adam Smith."

He took my hand and pressed something hard into it. "Aphra, I—"

"Seth!"

He pulled me close and brushed his lips against mine. "Remember," he whispered, and ran for the helicopter.

I opened my hand, and a lump rose in my throat. Seth's ring. Gold and garnet never looked so beautiful. I hugged the ring to my chest and waited for the pain I knew was about to come.

Seth climbed inside and closed the door behind him. The tug in my chest grew stronger as the helicopter lifted into the air, as if a part of me was attached to the runners and was slowly unraveling as they pulled away. But I didn't crumble as I had expected. If anything, I felt stronger.

A part of me *had* gone with Seth, but a part of him had stayed behind. It salved the growing ache, warmed me, made me smile. I slipped Seth's ring onto my finger, turned my face to the sky, and waved farewell.

epilogue

I was still standing on the landing pad when the authorities arrived. They weren't just police like Frank had said, either. When Junior crawled out of the helicopter, he was followed by three men wearing dark suits and serious expressions. They introduced themselves as CIA agents.

I may have forgotten to mention to the agents, until well after they had come down to the Plantation House and interrogated Darlene, my dad, and me, that the Mulos had left the island. The agency was not happy.... Especially when Watts filed his report. He claimed I had tried to poison him.

I never did learn where the Mulos went after they left our island. All Frank could say was that he dropped them in the city.

The doctors said Dad should make a full recovery, but it will take some time. Until then, he can't work, and he can't travel. He spends his days at the beach. Darlene is running the resort until he gets better.

I'm still going to see Cami ... or at least that's what Dad believes. As soon as she heard what I intended to do, Cami agreed to cover for me.

That paper Mrs. Mulo gave me? It was Mom's location.

She lives in Seattle.

I booked my flight today.

Intrigued?

Read Death by Latte
to find out what happens next
to Aphra . . . and to Seth.